Red Havoc Guardian

(Red Havoc Panthers, Book 4)

T. S. JOYCE

Red Havoc Guardian

ISBN-13: 978-1546644439
ISBN-10: 1546644431
Copyright © 2017, T. S. Joyce
First electronic publication: May 2017

T. S. Joyce
www. tsjoyce.com

All Rights Are Reserved. No part of this book may be used or reproduced in any manner whatsoever without written permission, except in the case of brief quotations embodied in critical articles and reviews. The unauthorized reproduction or distribution of this copyrighted work is illegal. No part of this book may be scanned, uploaded or distributed via the Internet or any other means, electronic or print, without the author's permission.

NOTE FROM THE AUTHOR:

This book is a work of fiction. The names, characters, places, and incidents are products of the writer's imagination or have been used fictitiously and are not to be construed as real. Any resemblance to persons, living or dead, actual events, locale or organizations is entirely coincidental. The author does not have any control over and does not assume any responsibility for third-party websites or their content.

Published in the United States of America

First digital publication: May 2017
First print publication: May 2017

Editing: Corinne DeMaagd
Cover Photography: Wander Aguiar
Cover Model: Tyler Halligan

DEDICATION

For Ty, aka Tyler Halligan, aka the other half of TnT. This book released exactly one year to the day that Bloodrunner Bear released. You remember that Ty? Our first project together, and now we're on number four. I can't wait to see what kind of trouble we get up to in the future.

Happy friendaversary.

ACKNOWLEDGMENTS

I couldn't write these books without some amazing people behind me. A huge thanks to Corinne DeMaagd, for helping me to polish my books, and for being an amazing and supportive friend. Looking back on our journey here, it makes me smile so big. You are an incredible teammate, C!

To my boybestie, Tyler Halligan, the model for this cover—hardworking steady-man who keeps me from fa-reaking out at events and before releases…I don't know what I would do without ya!

Thanks to Wander Aguiar and his amazing team for this shot for the cover.

To my cubs, who share me with the voices in my head. Thank you for being incredibly patient and always supportive and for bringing me surprise snacks on those big-work days.

And last but never least, thank you, awesome reader. You have done more for me and my stories than I can even explain on this teeny page. You found my books, and ran with them, and every share, review, and comment makes release days so incredibly special to me.

1010 is magic and so are you.

ONE

One name could change Greyson McCarty's entire life.

Genevieve. No last name was printed. Just her first name, and underneath the single word was another. Gorilla.

Greyson's hands shook, so he squeezed the paper harder to steady them. This wasn't how it was supposed to work. The Bangaboarlander matchmaking service he'd paid for was supposed to send him three options for a mate, with detailed information so he could decide if he wanted to meet any of them. And they were supposed to be doing the same with his information.

Greyson heaved a frustrated sigh and leaned back

into the leather couch in his cabin. With an irritated flick of his wrist, he tossed the thick cardstock paper. It floated and spun until it settled on his coffee table. What a waste of paper and a stamp. Bangaboarlander could've just sent him a damn email with those two words.

Genevieve. Pretty name, but he'd asked for a panther, or at the very least a big cat shifter to match his animal. He might as well have burned two hundred bucks.

Gorilla. What was she doing looking for a mate on a shifter matchmaking site? She should be in some family group somewhere under a big silverback.

His door swung open, and Greyson winced against the saturated sunlight that streamed around Barret's body. He had his hands on his hips and his pelvis thrust out.

"Your pants are unzipped, man," Greyson muttered.

"I know. I'm leaving it like that on purpose so Eden gets the hint and sucks my d—"

"What do you want?"

"Uuuh, I was just trying to tell you I want Eden to suck my d—"

"Barret, get the fuck out. Please."

"What's that?" The obnoxious green-eyed giant pointed a finger at the paper on the coffee table.

Greyson lurched forward and wadded it up in a ball as fast as he could. "Nothing."

"Genevieve. Gorilla." Barret had the most annoying smile on his face right now. His pants were still definitely unzipped, and he was letting the flies in and the air out the open door.

"Get out or come in, but shut the door!"

Barret stepped inside and then donkey-kicked the door closed like a child. Greyson had never wanted to punch someone in the throat so badly.

"What do you want? And if you mention your dick, I'm going to kill you." He could take Barret the Barbarian. The crew called him Murder Kitty, but they didn't know Greyson. They thought they did, but no one really knew him.

"You haven't paid us after the moonshine deliveries yet. Rent's due on the garage, and I need the money."

"Oh, shit. Okay, I'll be right back." Greyson rocked upward and tossed the wadded-up paper into the trash as he passed.

Down the hall in his room, he pulled open the lock box and counted out Barret's cut. He'd totally forgotten about crew payments. That's how messed up his head was right now. Before everyone started pairing up, he would've never missed a payment, but now all he could think about was finding a mate. He might not be ready, but his animal needed an anchor. He needed a female. He needed steady sex.

"Bangaboarlander dot com," Barret said from the doorway to Greyson's bedroom.

Fuck. With a soft growl, Greyson stood to face the crew idiot. "It was stupid, and it didn't work. They didn't find me a match."

"Oh my God, you want a mate?" Barret yelled.

"Shhhhhut the fuck up!" Greyson whisper-screamed.

As if Greyson hadn't heard him the first time, Barret turned super-freaking-annoying and mouthed it again. *Oh my God, you want a mate?*

"No." Greyson frowned. "Yes. Maybe. I don't know! You all look so happy and I'm alone and it sucks being single this long and yeah, okay, I have to listen to you all having sex every night because you're weird and loud and I want that sometimes."

"Loud sex?" Barret's face was all scrunched up and judgmental.

"No, not just that." Greyson shrugged up one shoulder. "I kind of want everything."

"So you went and got on Bangaboarlander? You know who runs that, right?"

"Yeah, Sebastian Kane of the Boarlanders."

"False, mother fucker. Willamena Barns of the Gray Backs. Jaxon's mom. The crazy one? She's who you trusted with 'matchmaker matchmaker make me a match…'" He sang the last part, the obnoxious troll.

"Well, no wonder I got a gorilla." Biggest waste of time ever.

"Wait, whoa, Mr. Prejudice. What's wrong with gorilla shifters? They're badasses."

"She's not a panther."

"So? Eden's a falcon. Kaylee's a lion. Jaxon's a bear. Anson's a puckered asshole."

"Are you done?"

"My point is, this crew ain't all panthers anymore. Look around you, Grey. We done mixed it up. It's a fucking zoo in these mountains now. Ben probably doesn't even cry himself to sleep anymore that we ruined his crew with other shifters. So she's a gorilla.

So what? The more important question…"

Taking him seriously, Greyson asked, "Yeah?"

"Is she hot, and are her tits size B or above?"

"God, I'm not having this conversation anymore," Greyson muttered, brushing past him and out into the living room. He opened the front door and held out a wad of ten dollar bills as Barret meandered into the living room.

As he passed Greyson, Barret snatched the money out of his hand, but stopped right in front of him, too damn close for comfort. "Grey, I strongly dislike you."

"Great."

"Like, sometimes I imagine ways to kill you."

"Fantastic."

"But also, it would be awesome if you were less of a grumpy prick."

"I literally hate where this is going."

"So, I'm going to give you some advice."

"Polite decline."

"Meet the gorilla. See what she's about before you decide against her. Give her lots of flowers. Girls love that shit. There's like…two million daisies right outside the door. Be sweet and get her addicted to you. At least see why Willa thought you were a match."

Huh. Barret was actually giving serious advice, and it was almost worth considering.

"And if nothing else, I'm sure gorilla shifters give great head."

Sometimes Greyson imagined ways to kill Barret, too.

As he watched Barret jog down his porch stairs, whistling happily to himself as he counted his cut of the moonshine money, Greyson had this urge to see if Barret had been telling the truth. Was it really Willamena Barns running Bangaboarlander? That would explain the poor match and the lack of information. He'd heard about her before, and not just from Jaxon, her son. She was a wild one and Second of the Gray Back Crew.

He pulled his phone from his back pocket and dialed Jathan's number. He was Jaxon's twin and Willa's other son.

"Lynn's still alive," Jathan answered. "You don't have to call every day, you know. If Creed got close to putting her down, I would call you, just like I said I would. Your whole damn crew is driving me insane with the constant calling."

"Is she improving at all?" he asked, ignoring Jathan's little tirade.

"Fuck if I know. She won't let anyone near her. She's bled everyone in our damn crew, and yesterday, Creed Changed and tried to put her panther in her place, but Lynn exposed her neck and begged for a kill bite immediately. Creed damn-near lost it on her." Jathan's sigh blasted static across the line. "Look, we're trying, but Ben's not giving us enough time on this one. A month is too short, and she's really far gone, man."

"It ain't over till it's over," Greyson murmured. God, he hoped Ben didn't have to put Lynn down. The crew would be gutted if they lost a member like that. Hell, if he was honest, he would really hurt if Lynn was killed. It would damage his panther in ways he couldn't understand or explain, but just thinking about her not being in his crew nearly gutted him. Every crew member was important to him, and Lynn had always been special. A little fragile, a little broken. She reminded him of a little bird that had broken it's wing young, but even crippled, had still tried to learn to fly. Some shifters weren't born strong enough for this life, and those were the ones that pulled at his protective instincts the most. "I have another question."

"I have shit to do."

"Your mom…"

"What about her?" Suspicion tainted Jathan's voice.

"Does she run Bangaboarlander now?"

Jathan huffed a laugh. "Please tell me you didn't try to get matched up with a mate on it."

Heat flooded Greyson's cheeks as he made his way to the trashcan. Thank God, Barret wasn't here to see him blush like a schoolboy with a crush. "Look, I need to know if the match she set up is bullshit."

Jathan's sigh tapered into a growl. "Look, I want nothing to do with any of that. Love is a crock of crap, and matchmaking is stupid. But my mom is a sappy romantic, deep, deeeeeep down in her weird little soul, and so if she matched you up with someone, she probably had a reason. Now piss off, Grey, and tell the rest of your crew to stop calling me. Lynn is the same, just like every other day. Stop hovering and give us space to try and help her."

When the line went dead, Greyson bent over, pulled the wadded-up paper from the trash, and uncrumpled it.

Barret and Jathan had both told him to give Genevieve a chance, and maybe there was something to that. He *was* curious…

But when Greyson imagined a lone, female gorilla trying to fit into this fucked-up crew of mostly big cat shifters, he shook his head and changed his mind. He couldn't do that to a shifter who was used to a close-knit family group.

And back into the trash her information went.

TWO

Gen's hands were shaking so badly she had to grip the steering wheel harder to still the tremble. This was the most terrifying thing she'd ever done—starting over.

She couldn't force her foot down on the gas pedal, no matter how hard she tried. So here she sat, staring at a dilapidated fence that declared the border of Red Havoc territory. There were signs riddled with bullet holes.

No trespassing.
Turn back now.
Fuck off.
No humans allowed.
Poachers will be poached.

Enter only if you don't value your limbs.

The messages were each hand painted on old, rusted-out sheets of metal that stretched as far as she could see down the fence. They were warning her to turn back and make a different decision, but she was already too far into this.

Her phone vibrated on her lap, and the light on the top blinked bright red to attract her attention. Gen checked the message. It was from her older brother, Torren.

I know what you're doing right now. You're freaking out, because that's what you do. Don't turn back. Turning back will put you under Sean again. No more being drained, Little Monkey.

She smiled at the childhood nickname he'd given her and scrolled down to read on.

I'm taking care of Sean and the others. Beaston called Red Havoc the Crew of Two Wars. One of those won't be yours, Gen. The gorillas won't come after you. Tell Dad...fuck, I don't know. Tell him I did what I had to do to keep you safe. He can't get involved in gorilla politics, and I have to make sure you steer clear of this too. Find a crew, Gen. Find something like we had growing up. Find happiness. If Greyson McCarty isn't it, try Bangaboarlander again and again until you find a safe haven. You're beautiful, strong, and just need time with normal shifters. You'll be all right, I swear. I'll call you in one week. If I don't, explain everything to Mom and Dad. Not until then though. I need that time to demolish that fuckin' family group for what they took from you. None of that was your fault, Gen. You were right to leave. You're stronger than you think. Love you.

Shhhit. Torren was going after Sean? Gen slammed her head back against the seat and closed her eyes at how messed up everything had become. Torren was a monster, and the only son of Kong, but he wasn't just going to challenge one silverback. He was going after the entire family group that had hurt her. Females were brutal, too. He was a good brother, but he was also reckless and had no family group under him to anchor him to this world. He'd become too mature, too dominant. Sure, he was keeping her safe, but he also needed fights like this to stay steady. She couldn't pull him off this battle if she tried.

Not her fault? Bullshit. She'd messed up in her choices, and now Torren could be hurt or worse by her bad decisions.

As much as she wanted to beg him to change his mind, it would be a waste of time. She'd learned that growing up. Silverbacks were stubborn in general, but Torren was something else. He'd never been moved on a decision, not once in his entire life. So instead she typed out, *Love you too, Big Monkey. And thank you for everything.* Send.

She glared up at the signs again and sighed. She owed it to Torren to try with Greyson. Her parents didn't even know she'd left Sean's family group yet. They didn't know anything about what went down. She'd been quiet about the struggle with everyone but Torren. Why? Because Dad was mother-fucking Kong, Alpha of the Lowlanders right outside of Damon's Mountains. He would've rained hell and sicced the blue dragon on that family group of gorillas. He would've torn Sean limb from limb and watched with a big fuckin' grin on his face while Damon Daye devoured their ashes. It would've started a war between gorillas and Damon's Mountains, and she couldn't be the cause of that.

She eased onto the gas and coasted through the open gate to Red Havoc territory. No turning back now. She had to at least see why she'd been matched with a panther shifter on Bangaboarlander. She'd memorized his information.

Greyson McCarty. Registered panther shifter. No mother. Father in shifter prison. Protective naturally. Bottom of the Red Havoc Crew by choice. Known likes: (and this is where things got weird) *boobs, olives, blue crayons, juice boxes, sixty-nines, long walks in the woods at midnight, tree-sex, green M&Ms, morning diddles, chocolate ice cream with chocolate sprinkles, asparagus. Not good at talking or sharing because panthers are assholes naturally. What he's looking for in a mate: a boss-babe who is cool with illegal shit, and again…boobs. Someone to make him sandwiches when he gets off work. Just kidding, Gen, never make a man a sandwich unless he earns it. Also he wants like…seven babies. He's hot as fuck. Six pack abs. I'm hungry for tacos. Worms rule. Good luck.*

Because of that last part, Gen was ninety-eight percent sure Willa of the Gray Backs had taken over Bash's control of the shifter matchmaking site, and maybe Willa wasn't the most trustworthy on making a match, but desperate times and measures and all.

Gen's heart pounded in her chest harder with

every turn on the one-lane dirt road that led deeper and deeper into the Red Havoc Woods. It felt like an hour before she pulled to a stop in front of a row of cabins. They were all similar in size, but a little different. When she laid eyes on the first house, chills rippled up her forearms. It was a replica of the 1010 trailer she'd grown up around. Beaston no doubt had his hands in these mountains, and that made her feel a little better.

The information on Greyson had an address listed at the bottom. Cabin 6 looked like it was at the very end, so she eased her mustang down the pot-hole-riddled dirt road, her eyes on the cabins the entire time. Her ride was souped-up and the exhaust loud. She couldn't hear it, but she liked big exhaust because she could feel the rumble. Touch was everything. The panthers should hear it, but no one was coming out of the cabins. Not until she pulled up to Cabin 6.

As she eased to a rolling stop and put the car in park, the cabin door opened slowly and out stepped a man. No…out stepped a beast. He was as tall as her father and every bit as wide through the shoulders. Blond hair was swept up and messy on top but shaved on the sides. Tendrils of ink snaked down his neck and disappeared into the white, thin material of his T-shirt. Both arms were covered in tattoos, but she didn't spend time studying them. His eyes were what captured her. Piercing blue, steady on her, but empty. His head was canted as if he was a curious animal, but his mouth was set in a grim line.

He didn't approach the car, but instead leaned on the open doorframe of his home, arms crossed so his biceps looked even bigger. Fuck, he could give Torren a run for his money on size. She'd assumed panthers would be smaller. Leaner. As she turned the car off and stepped out, her heart was banging hard against her sternum.

This was where it was going to get awkward. If he didn't know about her disability, he could hurt her with his reaction. She'd been hurt a thousand times and had hardened her heart against the sting of that pain, but this felt different. This man was a shot at something steady, something safe, and she didn't want him to reject her right away.

Not for being deaf.

She wanted him to look deeper. People always forgot to do that, though, so she expected the worst.

Poker face.

If it doesn't work, try again.

Be brave.

For once, be fucking brave.

THREE

What the actual hell was this lady doing here in Red Havoc territory? Did she have a death wish? She was damn lucky Barret and the others were in town right now or she would've had a brawl on her hands at the front gate.

"Can you not read the signs. No trespassing," he gritted out as the woman approached his porch.

She had a piece of paper in her hands, and rudely, didn't answer him. Just climbed the stairs steadily and handed him the paper. Her hand was shaking.

Greyson narrowed his eyes at the familiar paper and snatched it from her hand. He read the first few lines out loud. "Greyson McCarty. Registered panther shifter. No mother. Father in shifter prison.

Protective naturally. Bottom of the Red Havoc Crew by choice. Known likes…" He shook his head in shock. "What the fuck? I didn't put any of this on the questionnaire." Realization hit him like a bolt of lightning. "Wait, are you Genevieve?"

She nodded, her chin tucked to her chest like a child in trouble, her eyes on his lips.

"Are you submissive?" he asked, his voice getting louder.

Another nod, and he was going to fucking kill Willa Barns.

"The main thing I asked for in a match was a big-cat shifter, and the second thing was she needed to be dominant. Submissives won't work in this crew. The females here are dominant she-monsters."

She shook her head like she was confused, and she was still staring at his lips. This was getting weird. Genevieve was here, standing on his porch, the exact opposite of what he'd asked for. His hands shook, but not from submissive nerves like her…from anger instead. Somebody had wasted both of their time.

Greyson scrubbed his hand down his three-day scruff and sighed. "Okay. Let me think. We both got played. I'm not mad at you. You don't have to be mad at me, but this isn't a match. I'm sorry you drove out here. I can give you…I don't know…gas money if you want it."

Genevieve frowned at his lips and nodded once. And then without a word, she spun and bounded off the porch. He watched her go and really looked at her. She was tall, only a few inches shorter than him, and fit. Her ass looked fantastic in those tight, dark-wash jeans. Girl did her squats, or maybe gorilla shifters were just built like that. Strong. She had that hourglass shape he found so damn sexy, and her dark hair was cut short in a bob. She had bangs that hung in front of her face and swept to the side, but her hair didn't hide her eyes. No, instead, they made the blue more vibrant surrounded by all that dark. She was wearing a black headband with dark jewels that matched her skin-tight black shirt. What was most surprising was the ride she drove in. That wasn't a rental license plate, so she really owned the royal blue '69 Ford Mustang with the black racing stripe down the body and the hood scoop. Someone had put big tires and shiny chrome rims on it, and the old car was clean. Even the leather seats inside were black with a thick blue racing stripe down the driver's seat. He'd heard it coming it. Sounded like damn thunder coasting through the clearing. Clearly someone had done some serious modifications to this car to get it sounding like a damn beast. Did she work on the car? She was interesting—he would give her that much. Rude, though, for not talking.

She got in her car, and he gave her a two-fingered wave. *Bye, Genevieve.*

But instead of driving away, she leaned inside and got back out, toting a suitcase like it weighed nothing. She slammed the door to her car and marched back up to the porch. His face probably had a dumbfounded look right now.

"What, no!" he said as she shoved her way past him and into the house. "Seriously, no! You aren't staying."

She ignored him like a champ, so he grabbed her suitcase handle and pulled.

Genevieve startled so bad her entire body jerked, and when her eyes locked with his, the terror there made him let go of the suitcase immediately. She retreated toward the wall, not giving him her back, her eyes dipping to the floorboards as she clutched her suitcase close to her body like a shield.

Her hands still shook badly, so he squatted down and exposed his neck. It had been a long damn time since he'd been around a submissive, and he'd forgotten how gently they needed to be handled. God, he was an asshole. "I'm sorry, I didn't mean to scare you."

No reaction. Her eyes were still on the floor, her back pressed against the wall next to the hallway. Genevieve inhaled sharply, and when she looked up at him, her eyes were rimmed with tears, her lips parted like she wanted to say something.

"What is it?" he asked low. "What's wrong?"

A tear streaked down her face, and her cheeks went red as she rushed to wipe it away. She shook her head hard, sidestepped into the hallway, made her way into his bedroom, and then shut the door with a soft *click*. The lock sounded a second later.

Greyson stood slowly, utterly stunned by the moment they'd just shared. Inside, his panther was snarling, ready to fight what had hurt her, but that made no sense. She was a stranger, and the only thing she needed protecting was from him. He'd hurt her somehow. Made her cry, and now he felt like shit.

Ben was gonna kill him, revive him, and then kill him again for bringing a gorilla shifter into the mountains. He needed to talk to the alpha of Red Havoc as soon as possible because Greyson couldn't kick her out now. He wasn't mean enough, and something was wrong with her. She was scared. The terror in her pretty blue eyes at just being touched said as much, and now those protective instincts Willa talked about on his information sheet were kicked up to level-red.

Bangaboarlander had been a huge mistake—for both of them.

FOUR

God, she was pathetic. The only daughter of Kong, hiding in a locked bedroom, too embarrassed to face her potential mate.

Greyson had looked totally shocked when she'd panicked. He'd startled her, though. Him grabbing her suitcase was unexpected—she hadn't known he was right behind her. It was times like this she wished so hard she'd been born normal, that she'd been born with hearing. She wished she had the same senses as all the other shifters, but that wasn't her path. She'd never heard her mother's voice singing lullabies at night to her and Torren, or Dad saying "I love you, Little Monkey," or the birds or the wind in the trees or thunder or fucking anything except her own voice if she yelled loud enough, and she hated the sound of it. It was thick and off-key.

Stupid silence. It had ruined her first meeting with Greyson. He probably thought she was a total nutcase now. And he would be right. She was. But it wasn't always like this.

On the bed, she drew her knees up to her chest and stared at her open suitcase. She'd meant to unpack, but the drawers were full of Greyson's clothes. She probably should've checked if the 1010 trailer was available before she moved in here, but she hadn't been thinking straight. When she'd seen the rejection in his eyes as he tried to send her away, she'd panicked.

Oh, Greyson was a monster kitty. He felt heavy, and so dominant, but he'd gone to his knees the second she'd startled at him grabbing her luggage. Why? Why would a big alpha male like him do that? It didn't make any sense. She was beneath him. The lowest-ranking member in the family group, she would be the lowest-ranking member here, too. And yet he'd knelt and angled his head, exposing his neck in submission to her.

No man had ever done that.

Gen made her way to the door and rested her forehead against the cold wood, hand hovering over the handle. *For once, be fucking brave.*

Inhaling deeply, she eased the door open and padded out into the hallway. Carefully, she peeked around the corner. Greyson was standing by a small island in the kitchen, a bowl of cereal in front of him, spoon lifted to his open mouth, his eyes on hers as he stood there frozen like a statue. There was a loaded moment that sparked like electricity between them before he broke it and turned his back on her.

For a split second, she was hurt, but then he pulled a bowl from the cabinet by the fridge. His lips didn't form a single word as he made a second bowl of cereal, complete with milk and spoon. With a quick glance at her, he exposed his neck again and slid the bowl toward her. A peace offering.

Chest heaving with emotion she didn't understand, Gen made her way to the small kitchen island and sat on the single barstool. She dared a smile of thanks to him, and then in silence, always in silence, she ate off-brand Frosty Loops with him, one slow bite at a time. He kept pace, and with each bite, his eyes softened. The wariness left his countenance, and by the end of the bowl, the corners of his lips were turned up ever so slightly in a smile.

"You have a nice smile," he said. His lips were easy to read. Greyson was a man who enunciated well. Bonus points.

She wanted to return the compliment. Even slight, his smile kept drawing her attention. Full lips under a blondish-red beard and straight, white, perfect teeth. His eyes crinkled in the corners, even when his smile was tiny. She bet he was stunning when he gave a big smile. But she couldn't return the compliment because she didn't trust her voice. Never had. So she ducked her gaze shyly and stood to take her bowl to the sink. She took his too, and rinsed them. She felt his eyes on her back, and when she turned around, he said, "You didn't have to do mine."

She shrugged. She'd done all the dishes for the family group. One bowl and one spoon was nothing, and he'd been kind to make her a snack in the first place.

"...to me?" he asked. She'd missed the first part, so she watched his lips and hoped he would repeat, but he didn't. He just frowned at her, confusion swirling in his piercing blue eyes.

He opened his mouth to say something, but before he formed a word, he turned suddenly to the door. His neck muscles twitched with words she couldn't see, and then the front door opened suddenly, so hard it banked against the wall. The man who came in looked furious. Blond hair, gold eyes, his heavy dominance filled the whole room and made him feel the size of an eighteen-wheeler instead of a six-foot-tall man. He was talking too fast, jamming his finger at her. There were others leaking into the house behind him.

For once, be fucking brave.

Gen ignored her bone-deep instinct to run back to the room and lock herself in so they wouldn't make her leave. Instead, she forced one foot in front of the other and stood by Greyson. He looked down at her, determination in his eyes. "It's okay."

He looked at the dominant man, probably the alpha, Benson Saber, if her research on the reclusive crew was correct. They were yelling at each other. She could tell by the bulging veins in the alpha's neck. There was another man behind him, smiling as he looked back and forth between Ben and Greyson. There were two other women, and then…Eden?

Shocked, Gen signed *hello* to her. Eden looked just as stunned to see her standing in the small cabin, too.

"Gen?" Eden grinned so big as she ran for her.

Eden lifted her off the ground like they used to hug when they were growing up around Damon's Mountains. A set of impossibly strong arms went around them both in their hug, and with one sniff, Gen smelled Jaxon. Jaxon was here, too? She was laughing like a lunatic. She probably sounded like one, but fuck it. Her friends were here. This wasn't so scary now.

Eden released her and signed in simple alphabet, *What are you doing here?*

Fingers flying with excitement, Gen explained that she was here to see Grey. When she turned to point at him, he was staring at her hands with a deep furrow to his brow. She froze mid-explanation. Oooh, that's right. He didn't know.

"You're deaf?" he asked.

Gen dropped her hands immediately at the disappointment on his face. Her stomach curdled with that all too familiar rejection. He was just staring at her, the cereal smile long gone, waiting on an answer, so she nodded.

He scratched the back of his head and took two steps back, and now he wouldn't meet her eyes. Anger flared through her chest like a wild fire on a windy day. In ASL, she signed, *Stupid boy*.

"I don't understand what that means," Greyson said, enunciating each word slowly. He was probably speaking at yelling volume too, like that would help.

Her disappointment yawned open like a canyon. She gave him her middle finger. *Understand this.* She shrugged out from under Eden's arm, and made her way back to the bedroom.

She couldn't hear what was going on out there, but she could imagine it. Jaxon and Eden would be sticking up for her. They'd grown up near Damon's Mountains together, and that created loyalty. She loved them for it, but it wouldn't matter. She was leaving in the morning.

The deep disappointment in Greyson's eyes flashed across her mind, and her hands began to shake again, but this time out of fury. She'd been so stupid to have moments of hope during their cereal meal. Hope that he was different and wouldn't judge her. Hope that he could be the one to keep her safe, give her a good life. Hope that she could do the same for him.

If it doesn't work, try again.

Tonight she was going to cry and let herself feel disappointed over the let-down, because it was okay to hurt for a little while. Even tough girls were allowed to cry sometimes.

But then tomorrow, she was going to wake up, pack her things into her Mustang, and then she would try again.

FIVE

He'd screwed up again. God, he couldn't stop screwing up with her. She was angry at his reaction, obviously. He'd been shocked, though. A deaf shifter? How did that even happen? They had amazing abilities to heal. It couldn't be from a childhood illness because shifters didn't get sick. Had she been deaf her whole life?

She'd slammed the door. He didn't know much about women, but a slamming door wasn't a good sign.

"Greyson!" Ben yelled. "Are you listening to a word I'm saying?"

No. "Of course. Yes," Greyson murmured, forcing his attention from the hallway where Genevieve had disappeared.

"Dude, you're a total chode," Jaxon said. Why was his face red like he was pissed? "Gen is literally the nicest person ever. She flipped you off. You done messed the fuck up."

"H-has she always been deaf?"

"Yeah," Eden said in a pissed-off tone. "Since birth."

"What the fuck is she doing here?" Ben asked, looking from face to face like everyone had lost their mind but him. "Seriously? Gen? Genevieve the daughter of Layla and Kong? Of the Lowlanders? You brought a motherfucking gorilla into my mountains?"

In a half-assed explanation, Greyson muttered, "I didn't bring her here. We just matched up on Bangaboarlander."

Jaxon snorted and pursed his lips against an annoying grin. "Only losers go on bangaboarlander."

"Correction," Anson said from where he was leaning on the front wall. "Only desperate losers go on bangaboarlander."

"I'm gonna kick all of y'all's asses if you don't shut up," Eden gritted out. "Obviously, Gen was on bangaboarlander, and she's neither desperate nor a loser. She's awesome. You," she said, jamming a finger at Greyson, "get a D minus for manners. I'm gonna go check on her."

"No!" Greyson rushed out, bolting for the hallway before she could get there.

"What?" Eden asked. "Why?"

"Because I should be the one to check on her." He wanted to go knock on the door so bad and apologize. Wait…would she hear a knock? "How am I supposed to talk to her?" he asked Eden.

"A gorilla!" Ben repeated, hands on his hips and a pissed-off glare trained on Greyson. He lifted his pointer finger. "Lions." His middle finger was up next. "Falcons." Ring finger. "Gorillas. Are you all going to get us in a war with every goddamned bloodthirsty shifter culture in America?"

"Yes," Anson answered with a grin.

"Shut up," Ben growled.

Jaxon raised his hand. "I'd like to point out that my mate is a panther shifter, so I shouldn't be in trouble."

"You're a grizzly!" Ben yelled.

"Thank you?" Jaxon said, looking confused, the idiot.

"All I wanted was a panther crew. Simple. We could hide, we could avoid registration. Not a single one of you listened when I initiated you into this crew. Panther mates only, or no mates at all. Now we've got a fucking menagerie!"

Annalise spoke up. "But I like grizzlies, not panthers. Jaxon's hot."

Jaxon winked at his mate. "Thank you, baby."

"Nope." Ben walked out. There was no more explanation, no more yelling. He just left, and his mate Jenny followed with an oh-shit look on her face. "Greyson, get her out of here by morning!" he yelled over his shoulder as he disappeared around the front of the house.

"How rude," Anson said, pulling his mate Kaylee close against his side. He kissed the top of her head with a loud smack. "Ben left the door wide open."

Kaylee yawned and snuggled closer to Anson. "Ben's going to kill us all eventually if we keep disobeying him. I think he's getting tired of being the C-Team."

"Why is everyone still here?" Greyson asked.

"Because we're bonding, asshole," Barret scoffed. "Geez, Greyson, when was the last time anyone even wanted to hang out in your cabin with you? You're welcome."

Greyson stifled the snarl in his chest. All he wanted to do was check on Gen. "Seriously, get out."

"Sometimes, I hate you," Barret said. "Come on, Eden, lets blow this popsicle stand. Hey Greyson, you asked how you talk to her? Why don't you use sign language? She already taught you your first words, Romeo." Barret stuck up a middle finger. "Fuck." He stuck up his other middle finger. "You." He turned with a flourish. "Murder Kitty, out."

Eden snickered as she followed her mate, like Barret was actually funny and not the most annoying creature on the face of the entire planet. Love was weird.

"If you hurt her, I'll kill youuuu," Jaxon sang as he was the last to leave. He slammed the door so hard Greyson's house rattled, and he barely resisted the urge to throw the entire kitchen table at the door. He was so freaking angry all the time lately, and it was their fault. Everything had been fine when it was mostly a bachelor crew. Then they'd started pairing up, and now they wouldn't stop petting each other, kissing and fondling and giggling, and fuck! Now

Greyson, for the first time in his life, wanted all that. Their fault. It was their fault Genevieve, or Gen as everyone seemed to call her, was even here. He'd done bangaboarlander out of sheer desperation to get his panther to stop shredding him from the inside out since they'd made him want a bond and a relationship a man like him had no business wanting.

Stupid Red Havoc. He'd picked the wrong damn crew, but what other choice was there? He was a black-marked panther with his only blood relation in shifter prison, and no one but Ben would've taken him.

He muttered a soft curse and made his way to the bedroom door. He knocked loudly, but she didn't answer, so he pulled the key off the top ledge of the doorframe and unlocked it. Please let her be decent.

When he pushed open the door, his heart sank to the soles of his work boots. Gen was curled up on his bed on top of the covers, her shoulders shaking as she made sad, little sniffling sounds. Fuck. Every tear she was shedding onto his pillow was his fault.

In an attempt not to startle her again, he walked slowly around the other side of the bed where she was facing the wall. She did jerk, and her eyes went wide, but she settled fast and covered her face with her hands. He didn't like her hiding from him. The sheet with his information was lying on the bed in front of her as though she'd been reading it again. With a sigh, he pulled a pen from the small writing desk in the corner of his room and sat on the edge of the bed, right next to her. Usually he wanted lots of personal space, but it was different with her. They were both in this together, kind of. They'd both been duped by Willa, and both had barely survived a crappy day trying to navigate these tricky waters of a forced relationship.

He started writing in tiny print on the back of the paper, and by the time he was almost finished, she was peeking out through her fingertips in curiosity.

I fucked up. It's okay that you're deaf. I'm not perfect either. Far from it, obviously. I don't know how to talk around females. Never had one to take care of before. I fuck it up before I ever get off the ground with a girl, so eventually I quit trying. I got on Bangaboarlander because an arranged match seemed way more possible than a love match for someone like me. Now you go. Why did you want an arranged match? P.S. I'm really sorry how I reacted.

Gen sniffed, so he stood and got her a box of tissues from the bathroom. He didn't know what this said about him, but Gen was really fucking cute when she cried. Cheeks all pink, full bottom lip poked out so far he wanted to bite it, eyes so blue they looked like crystals. Even her mussed hair was sexy. What he didn't like was the smell of her sadness. It made his panther want to defend her.

Gen read it twice. He knew because he watched her pretty eyes move back and forth over the paper then back to the top. A soft smile curved her lips. *I've never had a man apologize before*, she wrote in pretty cursive letters with hearts dotting her *I*s. *You surprise me. And then irritate me. And then surprise me again.*

It won't get any better, he wrote under her response. *There is a hundred percent chance I'll be horrible at being a mate.*

Me too.

He chuckled and pointed to his question again. *Why did you want an arranged match?*

The smile dipped from her lips immediately, and he had to fight the urge to scoop her up and hug her. What was wrong with him? He wasn't a hugger. He was a fighter. Fight everything, embrace nothing. Her vulnerability was tugging at all his instincts now.

He watched her scribble the pretty loops of her words. Watched the graceful arch of her hand. She was a leftie. Cute. Different. Gen was definitely different. Interesting. Beautiful. Broken. That part was easy to see. She cried too much to be whole.

She handed him the paper, but hesitated on letting it go, as if she didn't know if she really wanted him to read it. And now she wouldn't meet his gaze. Instead, she laid her head on the pillow and fiddled with a loose thread on the bedspread.

Nonchalantly, and just because he felt like it, Greyson scooted closer to her before he read.

I was in a family group. The females weren't nice, and neither was the silverback I pledged to. I was at the bottom, and I didn't want to be there anymore, but I didn't really have a plan for a crew either. I went on Bangaboarlander because I've seen it match some great couples before. I was hoping for it to work on me so I didn't have to feel like I was at the bottom of anything anymore. I don't want to be less-than.

Greyson read the last line three times. He knew all about feeling less-than.

"Can you read my lips?" he asked.

She nodded, eyes on his mouth.

Greyson held up the information on him. "Some of this is wrong, but some is right. My dad is in shifter prison." He made a ticking sound behind his teeth and shook his head. "I don't talk about this. You seem easier to talk to because…" Well, she couldn't repeat anything or talk shit about his family.

Because I'm deaf and quiet, she mouthed.

He expected anger in her eyes, but her vivid blue gaze was steady, open, curious.

Honesty was best. "Yeah."

What did he do? she asked, forming each word slowly. Her lips were pretty. Soft, full, colored with some petal-pink lip gloss that matched the blush in her cheeks.

Greyson swallowed hard. "He killed someone. It was a challenge for Alpha that had been brewing for a long time. Only it happened in public. It was an uncontrolled Change for both my dad and the man he ended up killing. It was bad. Bloody. It wasn't an easy death, and there were human witnesses. Human law enforcement got involved. He's got two more years. I visit him every couple of weeks. He's been in there since I was seventeen." Greyson clenched and unclenched his jaw. "The sins of my father followed me. The crew I grew up in banished me immediately, and no crew would take in the son of the man who had killed another shifter in front of a human crowd. I wasn't good enough for a long time. I thought you should know the bad, so you can run if you want to." Greyson shrugged a shoulder up and dropped it again. "I thought you should know I am also less-than. I understand."

Genevieve sat up and wiped her damp cheeks. With a sniff, she straightened her spine and sat cross-legged, stuck out her hand for a shake. *I'm Gen.*

Greyson stared at her hand for a moment and huffed a soft chuckle. He didn't deserve it, but she was offering him a start-over. He slipped his palm against hers and gripped it. Her skin was warm, and her hand wasn't shaking anymore. She wasn't scared of him now. Good.

He shook her hand gently. "I'm Grey."

Her lips curved into a stunning smile, and her eyes brightened. They sat there on the bed, two strangers locked in a handshake, embarking on the beginnings of something big, or something painful—it was impossible to tell which yet.

Either way, they were in this together.

SIX

Ever the early bird, Gen slid her headband into her newly straightened hair, careful of her drying nails, painted bright pink because she wanted Greyson to think she was pretty. She'd also filled her single suitcase with mostly lingerie because, admittedly, she was a hoarder of lacy things. The only problem was, she didn't have very many outfits and she'd been traveling for a few days to get here, so now she needed to do laundry. Last night, when she'd moved her stuff into the vacant 1010 trailer, she realized very quickly that there was no washer and dryer. So, on today's agenda, she would find a laundromat.

Also, admittedly, she was equal parts excited and

nervous to get out of the bedroom and see Greyson again. He'd kept his distance last night, disappeared until late, and came back in with no explanation. He'd simply twitched his chin toward the couch and mouthed, *You take my bedroom. I'll sleep out here.*

That was when she went directly into his bedroom, zipped up her luggage, and made her way outside. She couldn't have him sleeping on a couch while she took his bed. He'd caught up to her before she even got off the porch, and this time, when he pulled on her luggage, she let him help.

Gentleman that he apparently was, he led her to the 1010 singlewide trailer like he knew her mind, and even ushered a little mouse out of the bedroom when she balked. Probably because she'd jumped up on the bed like a fraidy cat. She couldn't help it. She was tough about most things, but mice scared her on some primitive level. They always had.

Before he'd left last night, Greyson had looked as though he wanted to say something. His eyes had gone serious as he helped her off the bed, one hand on hers to steady her, one behind his back in a formal and stiff gesture. He frowned and parted his lips, but seemed to change his mind. The second her feet had hit the floor next to the bed, he'd pulled his hand away from hers and nodded a goodbye, turned and left her staring after him.

With each encounter, Greyson surprised her. The shifter boys she'd grown up with were cocky and loud. Abrasive almost, and Sean, the silverback in her family group, had made her distrust men altogether. But Grey was quiet and reserved, but with steel in the way he carried himself. And he was nice to her, sensitive to her submissiveness, and caring in little ways. Like helping her from the bed, making her cereal, and carrying her luggage. He did things for her without boasting or trying to get brownie points. He just did them.

Being deaf sucked balls, but there were advantages to it, too. She'd become a great observer and had a sixth sense whether people were good or not by the little things they did—how they held eye contact, the softness of their gaze, the empathy on their face if someone was in trouble. But even if she could tell Grey was a good man from all those things, the fact that he'd exposed his neck and tucked his dominance away just to make her more comfortable proved there was much more than met the eye with him.

Even in the span of a single day, she could tell he was different from any man she'd ever met.

Gen made her way out into the living room and smiled at the sack of groceries that sat on the table. When had he gone shopping? Were stores even open this early?

Inside the sack was a plastic container of cinnamon rolls, a loaf of bread, and a six-pack of bottled waters. When she turned on the faucet, she quickly figured out why the water was included. The tap water came out a stream of brown. Gross.

She opened the fridge to see a new gallon of milk, a carton of eggs, lunchmeat and cheese, and a small squeeze bottle of mayo.

She smiled as she hugged the mayo to her stomach. Without her asking, he'd fed her.

For the excuse to see him, she replaced the condiment and made her way out the front door to thank him. Only when she stepped onto the front porch, something horrifying was happening in front of the cabins, in a field of tiny white daisies. Two massive coal-colored panthers were in a battle that looked like it was to the death.

Shaking in shock, Gen bolted across the porch, but Jaxon stepped in front of her before she made it down the stairs, warning in his eyes as he shook his head. *Greyson and Ben have to do this. Grey broke rules.*

What rules? she signed in simple alphabet.

Eden answered from where she stood beside the porch railing. *Ben said you had to be gone by this morning. Greyson told him to literally fuck off. He said he was keeping you for another day. It's almost over, Gen. Ben has to punish him.*

Chest heaving, Gen watched in horror as the cats clawed, hissed, and bit, spinning time and time again until the dust was kicked up. The wooden railing under her grip began to splinter, but that couldn't be helped. She wanted it to be Ben's neck in her grasp.

Her inner gorilla was pulsing with power, begging for her skin. The fight dragged on for eternal seconds and, with each one that passed, it grew impossible to keep her skin.

Jaxon grasped her arm and was yelling something, but she didn't give a fuck about his words. He could keep them. Her body exploded, and the pain of the Change made the edges of her vision collapse inward. There were no Red Havoc woods anymore, no cabins, no sky, no grass. There were only the two panthers as she charged on all fours, and fuck the consequences of going rabid-gorilla on an alpha. The iron scent of Grey's blood filled the air, filled her nose, filled her lungs.

One of the cats sank claws and teeth into the other's back. Was it Grey with his lips curled back in a scream of pain? Or was it Ben?

Her knuckles blasted across the ground as she ran for them faster and faster. Who did she save? Who did she kill? There was no gray area for the gorilla. There was only red rage flooding every cell in her body.

The cats disengaged, and the injured one ran for the woods.

Gen skidded sideways to a stop, her hands and feet making deep divots in the dirt.

The triumphant panther stood there tall and proud, chest out, eyes blazing gold, lips snarled back. It roared at her. Or screamed? She was the daughter of silence. His warnings, his fury, his bellow of vengeance, were wasted on ears that didn't work. Definitely Ben. Grey wouldn't have pulled that.

Pissed, she slowly sidestepped toward the woods Grey had disappeared into, never taking her eyes from the alpha. Oh, she may be submissive, but that didn't count when someone messed with one of her people. And Grey was apparently one of those to her animal. He was a stranger. He was her people. Stranger. Mine. My stranger. Confusion swirled in her head and chest.

What was she doing? Charging the alpha of the crew wasn't going to win her a place at Grey's side.

Slowly, she gave the massive cat her back, watching him out of the corner of her eye as she walked to the edge of Red Havoc Woods where Grey had disappeared. She didn't need hearing to find him. The ground was speckled in crimson. A drop there on that dry leaf, a drop over there on that patch of moss, four drops on that stump in the middle of the path.

The storm clouds hid the early morning sun, and the wind kicked up, urging her on faster. She went to the trees where she was comfortable. After rushing up one, she bolted across a thick limb and jumped, reaching for a branch on the next tree that would bear her weight. This was instinct—moving through the canopy like this. It was hand-over-hand, not thinking, not slowing, searching the ground for Grey. *God, let him be okay.*

There.

He lay across a moss-covered felled tree, licking deep claw marks that had shredded his forearm. His eyes were on her, but he didn't stop cleaning the injury. When she moved to drop down to the forest floor, he curled his lips back and showed long, white, curved canines. So, she changed her mind at the last second and stayed put, high above him.

She didn't like people seeing her hurt either, so she got it. She understood, but she still couldn't force herself to leave.

Helpless to fix Grey's hurt, Gen pressed her back against the tree and, twenty feet off the ground, forced her body to relax. One leg dangling down off the limb, she quietly watched Grey below.

A few minutes passed before he stood and limped back in the direction they'd come. Gen dropped to the ground and followed at a distance. He never turned around to look at her, but he must've known she was there. Not once did he speed up and try to get away from her like Torren always did when he was hurt. Grey kept a steady pace until they reached the edge of the clearing with the cabins. He sat down, his long, black tail twitching in agitation.

Confused, she walked a few paces into the clearing toward 1010, turned, and waited for him. He only stared back at her with troubled, golden eyes.

Twitch, twitch, twitch. His tail swished through the leaves, but Grey didn't move to follow.

Gen made her way to the trailer and looked back, but Grey was gone like he'd never existed at all. Grey Ghost.

He'd run like Torren after all, but he'd done something utterly baffling first.

Even hurt and angry, Grey had walked her home.

SEVEN

Be brave. For once, be fucking brave.

Gen lifted her fist and knocked on the door. She had no idea how loud it was, but she did it hard so Benson Saber would be sure to hear it if he was inside.

The blond-haired, blue-eyed, pissed-off looking alpha yanked the door open before she even got the third wrap out. She startled hard and took a step back, averted her eyes, and exposed her neck like Sean had liked her to do.

There was a little boy, about six, peeking around his legs. He looked like his dad and smiled shyly before he wiggled his little fingers in a wave. Gen tried to smile, but it probably looked like a lip tremble. *Be brave.*

She exhaled a shaky breath and handed Ben the note she'd written. He waited two seconds too long to be polite before he yanked it out of her hand and unfolded it.

Gen imagined the words as he read it.

I want to ask Greyson out on a date. I'm not trying to cause trouble for your crew. I only want to find my place, and I don't want to leave until I rule these mountains out.

When she dared a look at his face, he was staring back at her. Oh, his eyes were still full of sternness, but his jaw had loosened from his earlier agitation. Ben reached behind him and cupped his son's head as he leaned on the open doorframe. Panthers seemed affectionate. She didn't know much about them, but she'd been watching today out the window of 1010. The mated pairs were always touching, but the males in the crew did, too. They gave quick hugs as they passed, or choreographed handshakes, or they rubbed shoulders.

There was one who felt off to her. Barret felt like he was maybe sick in his head, but he seemed to settle right down when he rubbed his cheek against one of the other males as they embraced.

Gorillas weren't like this. It confused her.

"Are you in trouble?" Benson asked.

She didn't know how to answer. Torren was trying to take care of the trouble that followed her, but she still had six days before he would call and tell her everything was okay. Maybe.

Benson looked down at his cub and bit his bottom lip. After a few moments, he asked, "Will you put my crew in danger?"

Shit. Well, she couldn't lie. She couldn't say for sure her old family group wouldn't come after her. Sean was like that. If he couldn't keep a female, he didn't want anyone else having her either. It was a silverback thing, and Gen had run in the middle of the night. So in answer she shrugged in an I-don't-know gesture.

Benson's eyes flashed gold and then back to blue again. "Why did you come after me when I was fighting Greyson?"

She wanted to tell him by using ASL. She wanted to do the explanation justice. Wanted to make him understand so he would let her stay, but he didn't understand sign language.

She pulled her phone out of her pocket and typed out a response as fast as she could so he wouldn't lose any more patience with her. *He has been kind to me. He feels important, but I don't know why. When I saw you fighting him, it felt like my fault and I didn't want him to be hurt. I don't know him well, but I know this...he would protect me too. I don't have anywhere else to go.*

And then she handed the alpha the phone and waited for him to finish reading.

"You could go back to Damon's Mountains," he said.

She couldn't get into why Kong, her father, couldn't get involved in gorilla politics. He'd fought so hard to be free of them, and he was outside of Damon's Mountains, the silverback of a small family group that included her mother and grandmother. He was a marked silverback, like Torren, with a long birthmark down his back that said he was supposed to be running the biggest and most powerful family group of gorilla shifters. Dad was happy, and could keep his quiet life as long as he stayed out of the gorilla world. If she involved him, he could lose everything. For her family's protection, she needed to find sanctuary away from Damon's Mountains. How did she explain that to Benson Saber, though? He was a panther and didn't understand gorilla culture. So she shook her head and shrugged. *I. Just. Can't.*

"That's not good enough for me. You can stay through the night, but tomorrow morning, I want you gone. It's nothing personal, Gen. I know who your father is. I respect him. But you could put my crew in danger, and we're up to our teeth in potential war as it is. I can't pick a fight with the gorillas right now. I wish you luck finding a place, but it's not here."

That last sentence felt like a punch in the gut.

Her place was nowhere. She'd left Dad's family group for a bigger one with a silverback who had tricked her. She hadn't ever belonged there, and now she was out in the world, spinning her wheels. And not only that, but the thought of leaving Grey made her stomach hurt. No, she didn't understand why. She didn't know him other than what she'd gathered in their small time together, but still, her eyes burned at the thought she would never get to know more of him.

Be brave.

She nodded jerkily and took her phone from his

hand. Without looking back, she made her way to 1010.

Grey hadn't come back. She'd watched for him, but he was still in the woods, and she couldn't just sit in the trailer all cooped up. On the inside, she felt volatile and unhappy, and she didn't want to be around Eden or Jaxon like this. Laundry still needed to be done, even if she was kicked out of Red Havoc territory, so she tossed her clothes into a trash bag from under the sink and shoved the two other potential mate information sheets into her purse. Bangaboarlander had given her three options, but she'd stopped looking after she'd read Grey's sheet. Something about him had drawn her here to the Appalachian Mountains. She believed in signs, believed in the power of instincts, and she'd owed it to herself to see why the words on a paper made the tightness in her chest ease, even if just a little bit.

Feeling at her lowest, she got into her Mustang and pulled away from the cabins, watching them disappear in her rearview. Tomorrow she would leave before dawn so she didn't have to say goodbyes. In the darkness, it would look different from the row of quaint cabins sitting in the shadow of two mountains behind them, surrounded by lush, green woods. This could've been her place. She could've settled in a simple home like this. It reminded her of the mountains she grew up in, but here, Ben was king of Red Havoc, and she was an outsider. Always an outsider.

The entire half hour drive to town, her thoughts stayed melancholy and frustrated. Covington, Virginia was tiny and only had one laundromat, right on the main drag, so it was easy enough to find. And thank goodness for small blessings, because Gen was distracted enough to get turned around easily on the unfamiliar roads. After parking, she fed dollars into the change machine inside, bought detergent packets, and sorted her clothes into two washers. The place was cute. It had daffodil-yellow walls and wainscoting. Usually the laundromats she used were a sterile white with dingy tiles and dust bunnies everywhere, but the lady at the front desk seemed to really love and care for her little business. She chatted with anyone who came close, and even gave a coloring book to a three-year-old girl who was running up and down the two aisles and stressing her mother out.

Unable to help herself, Gen smiled every time the little girl passed, who was clutching her coloring book and a three-pack of crayons as she ran. Gen wanted kids, but hadn't wanted them with Sean. Being in a big family group was so different than she'd imagined it would be. She'd grown up outside of Damon's Mountains, looking in and wishing she could be a part of a big crew like that. So, a big family group of gorillas was the dream growing up. She'd thought it would be fulfilling contributing to a community, and her gorilla had craved being coveted by a silverback. But within two weeks of pledging to Sean and his family group, she realized how wrong she'd been to join. Gorillas weren't like the shifters in Damon's Mountains. They were cutthroat, competitive, and brutal to weak links, like her. Because of her disability, she'd been shoved to the bottom of the group on day one, and the family group had made a constant game of putting her in her place.

In the laundromat, there was an older couple sitting together in the corner, laughing over a story the woman was telling. There was a man with a beer gut and a shirt that read *It's five o'clock some-bear* with a cartoon grizzly drinking out of a pitcher. The man was leaned back in his chair, most likely snoring from the look of his wide-open mouth, as his clothes tumbled on in the dryer in front of him.

Gen had always liked people watching. Good thing too, since talking to people was hard. Usually when they figured out she was deaf, they looked uncomfortable and moved away, so somewhere along the way, she'd stopped trying to converse.

There was another thirty minutes left on her clothes before she could move them to the dryer, so she pulled out the two information sheets from Bangaboarlander. The first one was about a thirty-year-old boar shifter named Jeremy Gordon. Still lived in the same town as his parents, wanted three piglets, liked steak and potatoes, and worked a nine-to-five, didn't like sweets, or booze, or curse words. It was like Willa had tried to make him sound boring.

Gen looked up as she flipped the page, and a familiar silhouette grabbed her attention. Greyson was standing across the street, a bag dangling from his hand as he talked to a pair of giants she didn't recognize. One had bright gold eyes and claw scars down his face.

Slowly, she stood and made her way to the large

window in front. Those weren't Red Havoc Panthers, though she would bet her boots they were big cat shifters. Tigers, or lions perhaps. She dipped her attention to the scar-faced man's lips and began to read his words as best she could.

If you don't, you know what'll happen. I'm losing my patience, and we're ready something something *retaliation. Cut us in or we expand our territory.*

Greyson's back was to her, so she couldn't read his part of the conversation, but from the tension in his shoulders and the aggressive gesture with his hand, he wasn't happy. Scarface was talking again, but Greyson shook his head hard, spun, and jogged across the street, giving both the shifters his back as he headed straight her way. He looked pissed, eyes so gold they were almost yellow, teeth gritted so hard his jaw muscles bulged. His fists were clenched, every muscle flexed. He ran one hand back and forth over his hair, spiking it up in all directions. Still looked sexy, though. He was muttering something that looked like "stupid mother fuckers," but she could've been wrong on account of how tight he kept his lips when he talked.

Grey hopped on the sidewalk and looked up,

locking eyes directly with hers. He jerked to a stop, and the anger disappeared from his face, replaced with shock. "Gen?"

Busted spying on him, she gave him a tiny wave while her cheeks caught fire.

Grey ran his hand down his beard and tossed a glance back over his shoulder, but the big cat shifters had walked away. Grey strode gracefully to the laundromat and pulled open the door.

"Hi," he said, approaching slowly, head canted and neck exposed slightly.

He was angry, she could smell it coming off him in waves, but he was still being sensitive to her submissiveness. Oh, she liked him.

"Oh wait." He frowned and made a clumsy sign for *hello* in ASL.

Gen couldn't help the giant grin that stretched her face as she signed the same back to him.

"Um, you look pretty." Grey shrugged and stared out the window, then tried again. "You look good today with your hair all shiny in the sun, and your nails have pink sparkles on them, and your eyes are a pretty color. Blue. I like your"—he gestured to her boobs—"shirt."

She laughed with noise, could feel the vibration, but got embarrassed when he stared at her lips, so she swallowed the sound back down.

"I like your laugh." His shoulders lifted and fell in a sigh, and he looked at the ceiling as if searching for inspiration. Was he blushing, too? "I wish I could sign and understand you."

Me too, she mouthed with a sad smile.

"I have a phone number. Do you?" He pulled his cell phone out of his back pocket. It had a black case, so she pointed to it and showed him her pink sparkly case. Opposites.

"I like black. It's my favorite color."

Pink, she mouthed through a smile.

"Girly girl?"

She nodded and showed him that her phone case matched her nails.

"You do good"—he pointed to her eyes—"make-up shit."

She almost laughed with noise again. She pulled his phone gently from his hand, typed in her number, and saved it as *BangaGen*.

When he laughed, the smile fell from her face with how badly she wished she could hear the sound of his voice. He texted her, *Hi BangaGen. It's BangaGrey.*

His blue eyes were dancing when she looked back up at him, and he'd taken a step closer to her.

She texted him, *I like doing make-up. Not just on me. I mean for a job. I do make-up and hair. Look.* Send. She pointed to her false eyelashes and then texted, *These aren't real. I do make-up for girls going to dances in high school and for brides, stuff like that.*

Grey was smiling really big now. When he took another step closer, their phones almost touched he was so near her. He typed out, *And you like sparkles?*

A lot, she mouthed. *Is that a deal breaker?*

He shook his head, eyes crinkling in the corners with his smile. "No. I think it's cute." There was a vintage soda machine in the corner, and he gestured to it and arched his blond brows in question.

She nodded, so he turned and led the way. They were glass bottles, and she chose an orange soda. He bought the same for himself and popped the caps, then tinked the neck of his bottle against hers in silent cheers. Always silent cheers. She wouldn't remember the sound of their first toast, but she would remember the vibration of it moving through her hand and up into her arm.

She gestured to the bag in his hand. The logo was of the Covington Bookstore. Grey shocked her to her core as he pressed his fingertips on her lower back and guided her toward a pair of empty chairs. Warmth spread from where he touched her, which made no sense because the fabric of her shirt separated their skin. In her stomach, there was a strange fluttering sensation. It was excitement mixed with growing feelings for the man who was now sitting down beside her. A part of her wished he would still touch her, and she didn't know how to flirt, so she took a risk and rested her hand on his thigh. He tensed for a moment, but his smile said he didn't mind, so she crossed her legs and left her hand right where it was because it felt comfortable and right. It had been a long damn time since anything had felt right.

You do make-up and I work weekend nights at a bar. Friday through Sunday night, I'm there until three in the morning. Sometimes later if I have to get the drunks home. And I deliver moonshine during the week. The real stuff, not the kind you buy at the liquor store. Are you a good girly girl? He didn't send that one, just showed her his phone.

She responded on her phone. *Oh, I'm definitely a bad girl. I got a C once in school, I snuck out of my house twice when I was sixteen, and I drank two screwdrivers before I turned twenty-one.* She showed him the message and beamed when he laughed reading it.

We are opposites, he typed into his phone. *I wonder why Willa only gave us one option...*

I got three. She showed him the message and then pulled the two pages from her purse.

On Grey's lips, the smile disappeared as if it never existed. His blond brows furrowed as he read her other options. And when he was done, he folded them carefully and tucked them back in her purse. His eyes were a muddy color, between blue and gold, and he bit his bottom lip as he watched a nearby dryer tumbling someone's load of towels.

She wished she could fix the moment she'd ruined, but right when she started typing out her apology, he turned to her and asked, "Do you want to go to lunch with me?"

Gen was shocked into stillness, and he repeated, forming the words slower. "Do you want to go to lunch with me?"

Like a date? she typed out on her phone.

Grey nodded.

Every fiber of her being wanted to say yes but... *Ben said I have to leave by the morning,* she mouthed.

"Let me take care of Ben."

She shook her head hard and typed, *I asked if I could keep you for a little while, just to see, and he gave me a hard no. I have to leave.*

Grey brushed her jaw with his knuckle, drawing her face toward his. Eyes locked on hers, he asked again, "Do you want to go to lunch with me?"

Yes.

The corner of his lips turned up in a smile. "Good. How do I sign that? Because this" —he pulled a book on ASL from the bookstore bag—"is really hard to follow."

Stunned, Gen took the book from his hands and dragged her fingertip down the spine. He'd bought a book to learn how to talk to her? In the year she'd lived in Sean's family group, he hadn't learned a single sign. And here was Grey, day two of knowing him, and he was already working to talk to her, on her level, not forcing her to read his lips forever.

Without thinking, she pulled his big calloused hand up to her cheek and rested against his touch, closing her eyes for a few moments just to enjoy the warmth of his skin against hers. When she opened her eyes again, he was staring at her face with a soft look that made her stomach flutter again. He rubbed his thumb right under her eye, and for a moment, she thought he would kiss her, right here in front of everyone in the laundromat. The old Gen would've balked and become embarrassed with public displays of affection. But right now, she wanted his lips against hers more than she'd ever wanted anything.

Instead of kissing her though, Grey said slowly, "I thought gorillas weren't affectionate."

Gen shrugged. Maybe watching the panthers be so affectionate with each other earlier today had made her hungry for touch. Or perhaps it was Grey's inner panther calling to her loving instincts. Or perhaps she was a broken gorilla in lots of ways.

"Today, when you charged into my fight with Ben…" He cocked an eyebrow and pulled his hand away from her face. "You can't do that again. We weren't finished, and I had to pull out of that fight so you wouldn't get hurt. Ben's still mad. We didn't work through my punishment. That being said, seeing you charge in there to help me..." His lip snarled up, and he suddenly looked hungry. He leveled her with a look and gripped the back of her neck. "You're. So. Fucking. Sexy."

Gen's heart stuttered in her chest at the intensity in his eyes. No one had ever called her sexy before. She wasn't a lithe white tiger shifter, or graceful flight shifter. She was a powerful female gorilla, and the boys in Damon's Mountains hadn't exactly been lining up to get in her panties. But without a shadow of a doubt, Grey meant what he was saying. He found her attractive.

She didn't like men being rough with her in general, but holy shit, she loved his firm grip on the back of her neck, forcing her to look at him right now. She gave a slow blink and a silly drunken smile right before he released her. Leaning back with a hot-boy smirk, Grey took a long sip of his drink, eyes never leaving hers. Losing her damn mind to hormones, Gen slid her hand to the inside of his thigh, and Grey's reaction was to roll his eyes closed and rock his hips ever so slightly, encouraging her, and holy hell she'd never wanted to slide her hand down a man's pants in public this badly.

Gen's phone vibrated with an alarm, letting her know it was time to take the laundry from the washer and put it in the dryer. And thank goodness for tiny blessings, because that alarm had just stopped her from going handsy-down-the-pantsy with Greyson McSexy Face.

She could feel his eyes on her as she worked, and twice she dared glances at him to find her instincts were spot on. He didn't even seem to care that she busted him staring. Grey was different from other men she'd been with. He was direct, confident, and didn't play games. He said what he thought, no beating around the bush with this one. It was refreshing.

Ben had told her she needed to leave, but with every second she spent with Grey, he became more interesting to her. More important. She didn't know what would happen tomorrow, and it made her sad to think about leaving when there was such a bright spark between them. But for tonight, she was going to pretend they had eternity. She wanted to make believe she could keep him, but letting herself fall and trust like this after what had happened with the family group was terrifying.

Be brave. For once, be fucking brave.

Maybe it was reckless, and perhaps she and Grey didn't have tomorrow—but today, Gen was going to let her guard down.

EIGHT

Grey was a bad boy, but a good man. Gen could tell. She liked that he was a good balance.

When he made the sign for *bird* again, she covered her heated cheeks with her hands to hide her blush. They were walking to a fried chicken place a couple blocks down from the laundromat. Her bag of clothes was sitting in the passenger's seat of her car. Grey had carried it like a gentleman, but in the laundromat, he had stared at her stack of folded lace panties not-like-a-gentleman.

And now they were enjoying a very slow stroll through downtown Covington. It was sunny today, and the trees that lined the streets cast speckles of shade as they passed under the branches. Grey was bobbing his head like there was music playing as he signed *bird* to himself again. He didn't seem to care that the people they passed looked at him. She liked that. He did what he wanted and fuck everyone else's opinions. She hoped that would rub off on her.

She pointed to her ear and bobbed her head. *Music?*

Grey looked up and around, then pulled her by the hand to a door that had a sign for Jessie's Brewskies. She giggled at the name and didn't even care if she made noise or sounded strange. Grey only turned and gave her a beaming grin as he pulled her inside the dimly lit bar. It was midday, so there weren't too many people, and she could feel the beat of the song through the floor and in the air. Possibly a country song, and when Grey pulled her onto an empty dance floor, rounded on her, and smoothly pushed her back into a two-step, she knew she'd been right. Definitely a country song.

Grey pointed to the speakers that lined the floor. "Beck Brothers." He looked at a young guy working the bar and nodded his chin in greeting. "This is where I work."

Gen stumbled and stepped on his toes. She hadn't

danced a two-step since she'd left Damon's Mountains. Dad had taught her at the bar her mom had managed. It was funny. Dad had two-stepped with her often while listening to the Beck Brothers play live music, and now she was dancing to one of their songs with a man who managed a bar, like her mom did. She'd grown up around a place just like this. There was this moment of deja vu, but it wasn't uncomfortable. It reminded her of home, and made her like this place even more.

Do. You. Work. Tonight? she asked carefully, trying to keep up with his dancing.

He nodded. "At six." He hooked a finger under her chin and stopped them. "Don't watch your feet. Watch me. Let me lead you. I'll take care of you."

Chills lifted the fine hairs on her forearms. She'd dreamed of a man saying something like that to her, but had never thought it would happen. On a whim, she mouthed, *I'll take care of you, too*. And she meant more than the dance.

Grey straightened his spine and pulled her one hand around his arm to rest on his shoulder, then held her other hand in a firm grasp. And there was this moment when they just stared at each other, electricity crackling between them. The bar faded away, and it was just them. The two of them and the beat that pulsed through her legs and landed in her chest. He nodded slightly with it, prepping her. One, two, three, and then he stepped her back into a two-step, holding her body close to his.

And they danced. Middle of the day, for no reason other than to have fun, on a random dance floor, matching smiles on their faces, her heart pounding to the beat of the music. She was happy. It was a warm sensation that flooded her entire body. Nothing else mattered but this, right here, being in his arms, being under his hands, being guided by him, lost in his smile. This was her favorite moment that she could remember, and Grey was the one giving it to her.

Maybe Willa had known what she was doing after all.

Again, like in the laundromat, she thought he would kiss her. At the end of the song, he twirled her like a pro, pulled her back in and dipped her. His face was so close, his eyes on her lips, but a soft frown took his features, and he pulled her back upright slowly without pressing his lips to hers.

He was holding back, and it confused her.

With a two-fingered wave for the bartender who was wiping down the counter of the quiet bar, Grey led her outside. But he wasn't touching her anymore. No hand-holding, no brushing his fingertips on the small of her back as he held the door open. In fact, he seemed to be keeping his distance from her.

The walk to the restaurant was uncomfortable. He didn't look at her, and she grew more and more upset. They'd danced and had fun and he'd called her sexy, and then he'd closed off fast.

Unable to stand this kind of silence, she tugged at his arm and stomped her foot, stopped walking. He turned on her, a question in his piercing blue eyes.

She typed into her phone, *What did I do wrong?* Send.

He frowned down at his phone and typed back, *Nothing.*

You won't touch me or look at me. I did something wrong. Send.

Grey gave her a blazing warning look before he started typing. *No, no, no, you're great. But when I grabbed your suitcase yesterday, you got scared, and I don't understand why you left your family group yet. I don't want to push you.*

I didn't get hurt by the silverback. Not like that. Send.

"Then how?" he asked.

God, she owed him an explanation, but she hadn't told anyone but Torren what had happened. She was so ashamed. So angry and sad still.

Swallowing her cowardice down, she typed out her embarrassing admission. *I want a cochlear implant. I'm a candidate. Hearing aids don't work for my kind of hearing loss, but if I got a cochlear implant, I could perceive sound. Not like you, but at least it would be something. I'm a shifter. We're not supposed to be disabled, so there's not insurance that will cover it for me. My parents and I had been saving up since I was sixteen and I decided I wanted one.* Send.

"How much?" Grey asked.

40. Send.

His eyebrows jacked up to his hairline. "Forty thousand dollars?"

Gen nodded and typed, *I had twenty-five saved up. I worked really hard since I was sixteen, and my parents did what they could. Even my brother, Torren, helped. I was getting closer…"* Send.

Fuck, she didn't want to put the rest. She was

supposed to be this powerful female gorilla, and she'd let a man take her hard work away. *Be brave.* She took a deep breath and continued. *Sean, the silverback in my family group, found out I had the money. They worked me for three months, bullying, fighting me, badgering me, saying horrible stuff, dragging me to my knees until I got so sad, I gave up the password to my bank account just to make them stop. They made me feel like I was nothing. Sean said that all the time. You're nothing. I got weak and gave in and Sean drained me. He took my money. All of it. The way he did it was really messed up. He knew it was for my surgery, and he stole it anyway. He said it was for the good of the family group, but two days later, he bought himself a new motorcycle with my life savings.*

She waited a minute, wishing she could delete it and tell a joke to lighten the conversation, but Grey had been honest about his dad being in shifter prison. He didn't play games. Send.

As Grey read her response, red crept up his neck and landed in his face. And when he looked back at her, his eyes were gold like the sun, with tiny pupils that made them look even more feral, and brighter. His face was twisted in fury. The air thickened, congealing in her throat like she was trying to breathe water. Oh, Grey was dangerous, and Gen was glad she wasn't the one who had caused his anger. Even now, every instinct in her body screamed for her to kneel down and expose her neck to him, and he wasn't even asking her to. Somehow, he was very good at masking just how dominant he was, but right now he wasn't pretending at all. She wouldn't want to cross a man like him. But him being angry on her behalf? It made her feel safe and cared for.

Grey looked back at his phone, re-reading she supposed, and shook his head. His jaw was clenched hard, and she expected him to act like Torren when he was pissed. Walk away.

He didn't, though. Suddenly, he snaked an arm out and pulled her flush against his stony chest. His face was pressed into her hair, and his body shook. He smelled of fur. And then it hit her. Grey was close to a Change. She tried to make a "shhhhh" noise and hoped it sounded okay as she slowly, lightly ran her nails up and down his back.

He was saying something. She could feel the vibration of his words rattling through his chest to hers, but she didn't want to pull away from him to read his lips. This felt so good, being all wrapped up in his arms. She'd been grieving the loss of that money alone. She'd put her hopes in that surgery, and now it wouldn't happen. She would always be the daughter of silence because a man who was supposed to care for her had wanted a motorcycle. She was disgusted with him, but also with herself for letting it happen. She should've protected her little treasure better.

And here was Grey, probably murmuring something soothing because that was him—caring. He was hugging her tight, angry on her behalf, and she didn't feel so alone with the shame and the hurt and the quiet fury. He was shouldering something big with her, and the weight on her chest and shoulders wasn't so impossible to carry anymore.

Gen lifted up on her tiptoes and buried her face against his neck. He smelled like fur and cologne. Like Grey. She memorized his scent. And then she pressed her lips over his tripping pulse. When she did, she realized he wasn't talking at all. He was growling. His inner panther was worked up. The vibration softened when her lips lingered on his throat. Testing, she parted her lips slightly and sucked, brushing her tongue against his skin. His hands went to her hips and dug in, dragging her body closer. The tenor of his snarl changed. Was he purring? She smiled into her next sucking kiss. Suddenly, he pulled back and took her hand and led her down the sidewalk toward the restaurant. Hot and cold, hot and cold, Grey made her head spin. But then right as disappointment was unfurling in her chest, he pulled her into a small alleyway between two buildings and pressed his back against the brick building. With a devilish smile, he splayed his legs until he was at eye level with her, and by her hips, he dragged her to him. His thick erection pressed against her, and now the flutters in her stomach were going wild.

Grey cupped the side of her neck, and for a split-second, right before they kissed, he hovered right in front of her in a sexy tease, giving her an option to run or not.

She wasn't running. Not from him. *Be brave.*

Gen leaned into him and sucked on his bottom lip, her hands splayed on his chiseled pecs. There was a soft groan from him. She could feel it through her hands and wished with everything she had that she could hear the noise he made. Bodies pressed against each other, Gen closed her eyes to the world and just *felt* him. Lips moving together, tongues touching, tasting, the scratchy sensation of his beard against her skin, his hands exploring her body. His fingers went up her shirt and dragged across the skin of her lower back, around her hip. God, she wanted him. Wanted him so bad. Wished they were back in 1010 so she could get to know his body properly. But maybe this was better, getting lost in a kiss without the promise of anything more.

His kisses had been meant for her. Made for her. His mouth moved against hers like he knew exactly what she liked. This was a man who was in control, but he'd taken the submissive position for her, his back against the wall. He'd allowed her to trap him so she wouldn't feel crowded. Ooooh, she liked him so much already.

He controlled the pace. Sometimes he went hard, thrusting his tongue into her mouth and gripping the back of her hair, and then he would soften his mouth against hers and slow them down. His hand would go gentle as he rubbed her back as though petting her, as though he was coveting her. And then slowly, the fire would build to an inferno, and then they were barely in control once again.

This was everything. It was feeling those first tingles of a bond she thought she would go to her grave never feeling.

But this wasn't supposed to work, right? Bangaboarlander was supposed to be a way for her to find an arranged mate she was friendly with, one who she could commit to, but loveless, like she'd done with Sean.

What she was building with Grey felt too good to be true, and it was. Because Ben had laid down the order that she couldn't stay.

NINE

Gen pulled away from their kiss suddenly and searched Grey's eyes with this look of fear on her face.

"What's wrong?" he asked, careful to enunciate his words for her.

I don't want to leave tomorrow, she mouthed.

Oh. That. Grey sighed and pushed her bangs out from in front of her eyes so he could see her better. "I'll take care of that. Don't worry. We're not done yet."

"Are y'all gonna do it," Whiskey Barney slurred from the mouth of the alley. "Cause if so, I'm gonna video it and make a million-trillion-billion dollar. Dollars. Dollars is a weird word if you say it a lot.

Dollars."

Greyson chuckled and shook his head. "Sorry, WB. No alley sex this time around. Better luck next time."

"Okay. Jessie said I'm cut off. He kicked me out."

"Well you sound three sheets to the wind, so that's probably best. How long did he say you're cut off?"

Barney burped and swayed on his feet, then ran a hand over his balding dome and gave a goofy grin. "'Till I sober up again."

"So forever."

"Pretty much. I'm gonna go to the old bar. They like the Barney show over there."

"Don't drive!"

"My car ain't even runnin'. I forgot to put gas in it," he slurred, walking away. "Over his shoulder, he called, "Your girlfriend is hot. Stay bad to the bone you wild and crazy…crazy…dollars."

Gen looked concerned and formed the words, *Is he okay?*

"Oh, yeah. That's just Whiskey Barney. He's one of the many characters of this town. He comes into the bar a lot."

A regular?

"Yep. Come on, I can hear your stomach growling from here. I wish we could stay right here and make out all night, but I have this instinct… I need to get you fed. Is that weird?"

Her smile turned so fucking cute, and pink painted her cheeks as she shook her head. She liked when he took care of little things, he could tell. Oh, she was tough. She had to be to live the life she had without being able to hear, and she hadn't let it turn her bitter. She was sweet instead. The world hadn't made her hard, just strong.

Gen was complicated. He used to think he wanted the simplest girl, the simplest relationship he could find, but this girl had layers and depth. She had everything. He hadn't found a single thing about her he didn't like.

He held out his bent elbow, and she slipped her hand into the crook of his arm. Her grip was strong. That unintentional strength was probably a gorilla thing, but he didn't mind. His body was made to be roughed up. He could handle her, and there was no doubt in his mind she could handle him, too. She might be shy and sweet, but Genevieve Taylor, only daughter of the legendary Kong, was anything but fragile. Sexy, sexy, little Lowlander. Grey had got so fucking lucky.

Gen was a beauty, but she didn't know it. That much was clear from the way she ducked her head and blushed at every compliment and from the way she avoided eye contact with people who looked or stared at her on the street. She probably thought they saw her as deaf, but how could they? She was stunning with her dark hair, light blue eyes, and her make-up done all pretty. He bet she was really good at her job and made women feel gorgeous when she did their hair and make-up. He was probably going to kill Sean. He wished she'd told him that douchebag's last name, but he would find it. When he got home from work tonight, he would get on the computer and track that prick down. Taking money from Gen. Taking surgery money? What a horrible person. Grey wanted to rip his throat out. Slowly.

Gen was looking up at him as they walked, her delicately-arched, perfect dark eyebrows in the cutest fucking little frown he'd ever laid eyes on.

You okay? she asked.

Huh. He liked how she made him feel when she

cared. She probably wouldn't appreciate if he told her he was imagining ways to murder her ex, so he put his arm around her shoulders and gathered her close to his side instead. She liked when he touched her. She always softened against him. Good mate.

And fuck Ben for trying to lay down the law when it came to Greyson. The alpha had let everyone else pick their mate, and then balked when it came to him? It was bullshit. Just because their pairing was arranged didn't mean it couldn't be something worthwhile.

Gen nuzzled her soft cheek against his chest as they walked, and it did something strange to his heart and his dick at the same time. Hard dick, soft heart. She was so damn easy to be around. Not just because she was beautiful, sweet, and interesting. But her being deaf? That was never a deal breaker. Sure, he'd been shocked at first, but he was quiet naturally and didn't need a woman who filled silence with empty words. He would never wish the disability on Gen, but she suited him just fine the way she was. Hearing impaired or not, it didn't matter to him. He would just learn how to talk her language, and that would be that.

The second they walked in through the door of the restaurant, he smelled the lions. Fuck. Seth, the new alpha of the Cold Mountain Pride, and Abel, his Second, were sitting at a table in the corner, staring at him. The second Seth's eyes slid to Gen, Greyson wanted to shove a fork in his eye.

He was completely distracted by the staring contest with those assholes as he followed Gen and a waitress to a table on the opposite side of the restaurant.

He had to rush to pull out Gen's chair before she sat down because he was in his own little world of wondering what the hell he was going to do about the pride. He needed to get his head back on Gen so he didn't hurt her feelings. She was more sensitive than him.

She started texting the second after the waitress got their drink orders.

Lions?

Smart girl, she had been watching through the window of the laundromat as he'd argued with the leaders of the pride.

He nodded and clasped his hands in front of his chin, debating on what to tell her. *We are on the verge of war*, he mouthed. No sound because Gen didn't need it, plus he didn't want the lions with their oversensitive hearing to catch wind of this conversation.

He texted her, explaining something he hadn't even told Ben or the others in Red Havoc. *We've been going back and forth with these battles. They're pushing into our territory, we're defending it, their last alpha came after Kaylee and her son, and now he's gone. Dead. There is a new alpha in the pride. When power shifts, it's hard on a crew, and right in the middle of that, two of our cats went after them a couple weeks ago. We got in a scuffle that should've never happened. It's their move now. I've been trying to slow the retaliation down without my crew knowing. The more people who get involved, the worse it is. I can't avoid war if I have Barret and Anson and Jaxon and even Ben pushing the pride to the edge.* Send.

She texted back, *You're like the Red Havoc Guardian, but no one knows.*

He huffed a breath and shrugged. *I guess. I've done quiet stuff like this since Ben let me in. Stopped battles from happening before they became an issue. The others are too loud. Too ready to fight. Too reckless. I want to keep the crew together, and safe.* Send.

Because you were kicked out of your crew when your dad went to prison?

He nodded. *I do best in a crew, and I like Red Havoc. They get on my damn nerves most of the time, but they're mine. Mine to protect.* God, he wanted to tell her she was his to protect, but it was too soon. He didn't want her to run if she saw how protective he already was over her. If Gen had been under a big domineering silverback in that family group and hurt by that, he didn't want her to lump him in with that kind of man. He wanted to be better for her. So instead of saying that, he typed out, *After I was kicked out at seventeen, the loneliness made my panther hard to manage. I don't want to go back to that, and no one else is going to take me in but Ben. Shifter memory is long, and no one has forgotten my dad getting that crew outed and forced to publicly register. No one forgot the video of him Changing in the middle of a bar parking lot and killing the alpha of our crew. He messed up, and it'll follow me for always. I'm okay with that, so long as I have a place in a crew.* Send.

After reading, Gen sighed and cocked her head.

Then she texted him, *What if I get you kicked out of Red Havoc? I don't want that.*

"You won't," he murmured, forming his words carefully. "Ben will have to just accept us eventually. Let me worry about him, okay?"

She still looked worried, so he brushed his work boots against her knee-high fashion boots under the table. So fucking pretty, looking all worried that she would get him banished from his crew. She was a protector just like him. A guardian. It was natural for her. He loved that about her. For the rest of his life he would never forget her charging into that fight with Ben, her powerful, black-furred arms punching the ground with every deliberate stride, her eyes blazing an inhuman silver, her smooth black lips curled back to expose long, curved canines that rivaled big cat shifters. So fucking dangerous. Powerful. Gorgeous. His.

"You're easy to talk to. I feel like I can confess things to you that I don't to other people."

You're quiet?

"Red Havoc bitches about it all the time, me being quiet. I just don't talk if I don't have something important to say. I think actions speak louder than words. I keep them safe quietly. I'm good with not talking."

Her full lips mouthed words as she typed the next text into her phone. She probably didn't even realize she was doing it. He wished he could hear her voice. Her laugh was different from any he'd heard, but it was perfect. It made him proud when he could make her smile like that and lose her self-consciousness.

His phone chirped with her message, and he read it. *I like that you talk to me.*

He inhaled deeply as the waitress set their drinks and food on the table between them. It was one of those old-fashioned family-style joints that only served fried chicken, mashed potatoes, biscuits, and corn. Gen started filling up her plate while he typed the next message. It was a long one.

The pride came to me a week ago, pressuring me to cut them in on our moonshine business. They want the profit. Not only that, but they want us to make bigger batches and expand territory so they have a big income coming in. They would assume none of the risk though. Red Havoc would. Right now, we make smaller batches and sell it to regulars. Locals. I know all of our customers and keep our risk of getting caught low, but the pride will get us caught, arrested, and human law won't go lenient on us. Making more means more illegal profit. We can't get caught doing huge batches or human law enforcement would use us as an example. I think the lions want that. They're playing the money angle, but there are only four males in the pride right now, and Red Havoc has been growing with females that could fucking annihilate them, even without the boys. Their only play if they want our territory is to use the humans to cut us out of the Appalachian Mountains.

By the time he hit send, Gen was handing him a full plate she'd made up for him. She didn't look for thanks or anything, just went to unwrapping her silverware. It made him grin. She was so much more comfortable with him now than she was even yesterday. He loved it.

It took her a while to read his text, and when she finally finished, she mouthed, *What will you do about the lions?*

Gen watched his lips, so he mouthed the answer. *I don't know. I'm stalling as much as I can. We can't up moonshine production without getting bad attention. They're threatening war, but right now, I'm banking on them being too small a pride to really come after us. It would be a stupid move on their part. We have a crew of monsters.*

Gen texted a quick response and started cutting her chicken off the bone like a girl with manners. Cute. He was going to eat like an animal and see if she ran. Test. She made him want to test if she would stick around when things went to shit, because they would. If it wasn't war with the Cold Mountain Pride, they still had a Dunn lion cub, Bentley, whose massive and violent Dunn relatives would come for him someday. And then there was Eden, Barret's mate. She was an albino falcon. Eventually her people would come for her too, and Red Havoc would go to war to defend its own. He could understand Ben not wanting to bring in a female gorilla shifter on the run. He understood, but it didn't change his mind. She had a place at Grey's side if she wanted it. If she passed his tests. If she stuck around even through the hell that would come for the Red Havoc Crew.

The little blue light on his phone was blinking, letting him know her message was waiting for him to read, so he did. *You could kill the lions. Problem solved.*

For a moment, he thought she was joking, but as

he stared at her, she just kept cutting up her food and eating, like she saw nothing wrong with making the problem disappear by way of death. He was going to have to do more research on gorillas. They were even more reclusive than panthers and hard to find information on. He was starting to think they lived by different rules than other shifter crews. More violent ones perhaps. And now he had the feeling that if he could get her to bond to him, Gen would be a true ride-or-die mate. No wonder she hadn't been scared off by his confession that his father was in prison. She didn't seem like the type of woman scared easily by inner demons. The more he got to know her, the more interesting she became. And now his inner panther was practically staring at her like a trained seal waiting for a fish. If he was good to her, she rewarded him with little insights to herself.

Sean had no idea what he'd let go, the dumbass.

As he watched Gen eat her food, Grey thought there wasn't much he wouldn't do to keep her safe and happy. Too soon? Fuck it. That's the way he'd always hoped it would work when he found a mate.

She was his now, and that was that. He just needed to convince her they were a match, and then he was going to burn her other two Bangaboarlander option sheets to ashes.

TEN

Gen pulled up in front of 1010 to find Greyson had beat her there and was sitting on the bottom stair of the small porch of the trailer. In his fingers, he twirled a little white oxeye daisy flower, and the butterflies in her stomach fluttered on.

She parked on the weeds and gave him a little wave as she turned off her Mustang. Grey smiled, but it didn't reach his eyes. Uh oh. What had she done wrong? They'd had a great lunch date, made out in the alley, and he'd talked with her for half an hour at her car before they'd parted to drive back to Red Havoc territory. What had changed from thirty minutes ago to now?

She pulled her laundry out of the passenger's seat

and made her way across the ankle-high grass to him.

"Nothing's wrong. I just…" Grey gave his attention to a pair of panthers walking the tree line side-by-side. His eyes were a muddy cross between blue and gold when he arced his gaze back to her. "I was offered a full-time manager position at Jessie's a couple of weeks back. I put off the decision because it will have me working almost every night, and I have to run the moonshine deliveries. I didn't have any reason to pile on more work before…but now things are different."

Why different? she mouthed.

"Because we have to start rebuilding your savings for your cochlear implant, Gen. What Sean did? It was sooo fucked up. But you still deserve the surgery if you want it. All I want to do is spend every second with you that I can, but I'm gonna take the job and I'm gonna up our moonshine production so I can bring even more in. Fuck the lions. This has nothing to do with them. It has everything to do with you. I'm sorry if it's too soon to talk like this, but it's how I feel. How my panther feels. I want to help you, take care of you, and keep you… It's an instinct…and I need to start bringing in more income because, someday, I want you to hear my voice. Mine first. I know that's selfish, but I don't give a fuck. I want you to *hear* me when I tell you how pretty I think you look, how valuable you are. And how kind, sweet, and strong you are."

Gen's face crumpled and her eyes burned. His offer meant more than anything in the world to her. This was the moment she chose him. Ben was kicking her out, but she would simply have to find a way to stay here with Grey. With *her* Grey. She reached into her purse as a tear streaked down her cheek and handed him the other Bangaboarlander matches.

Without a single second of hesitation, Grey ripped the pages to tiny pieces and left them in a pile on the bottom stair. And then he stood, handed her the little white flower, and took the bag of folded laundry. He was trading her, giving her something small and meaningful in exchange for the burden of the weight. How symbolic. How very Greyson—giving her something beautiful but taking the weight from her to put it onto himself.

Her inner gorilla was utterly stunned, and smitten. And possessive. Greyson had Gen's attention like no man had ever managed. He was a good-to-his-core man, and she wanted to keep him, too.

He led her into 1010. She didn't flip the light switch on because she didn't have a pleasant conversation with him on her mind. No, she wanted more. She wanted to touch him. Wanted him to touch her, because deep down she knew they would be bonded completely if he buried himself inside of her. And she was so worked up from earlier in the alley already, she just wanted that and more. She wanted to *feel* again.

Grey dropped the laundry bag on the floor near the hallway and then rounded on her like he knew her intentions. Like he could feel her stalking him. His eyes blazed gold as he strode for her, and then his lips were on hers, crashing like a tsunami wave. It would've hurt if she wasn't ready and wanting a little pain right now. Grey felt heavy, so heavy. Dominant, mature shifter, and how was he not an alpha? His intense, raw, primal dominance rivaled any silverback she'd met. She fucking loved the way he grabbed the hair at the nape of her neck and arched her head back to kiss her throat. Hard suck, then a lick and, oh my God, she was gone. She clutched his shirt with a gasp, then ripped it. Fuck the fabric, she needed to touch his skin. His chest rattled under her touch. Growl or purr, it didn't matter, he was so fucking sexy all riled up like this. He backed her toward a table by the door and shoved off a key bowl. It shattered on the floor, but Grey only smiled against her lips and bit her bottom one in a delicious tease.

Bossy boy, she loved him taking control. He ripped her shirt like she had his and tossed it on the floor, yanked her hands back to his pecs, and pressed her touch there as he kissed her. He gripped her hips hard and lifted her up to sit on the edge of the table. God, she wished she could hear the noise he was making right now. It rattled the air, vibrating against her skin and driving her mad.

Feeling bold, she eased out of the kiss and bit his neck, softly, teasing, but hard enough to say without words, "This is mine."

Grey jerked her hips into his so hard the legs of the table stuttered a few inches across the floor under her. She bit down as she spread her legs wider, creating a cradle he could fit into because she needed to feel his erection against her right now. He rolled his hips, and she met him, reveling in the sensation of him between her legs. His kisses were harder now, more desperate. His control was slipping, and she felt like a goddess. She felt like a vixen. Like she was beautiful. Greyson popped the button of her jeans and ripped them down her legs, kissing her so hard her lips throbbed. His gold eyes flashed with hunger as he stared down between her legs, and the smile on his lips turned devilish as he slid his hand to her sex and pushed two fingers inside her.

She curled her toes and arched back, gasping at how good it felt. He stroked his fingers into her slowly, torturing her until she cupped his hand and encouraged him to go faster. Grey lifted her hand and bit her right by the thumb. Punishment, but his smile was still there. It was feral, sure, but it was there, and it counted. He knew how to play, but she'd been close, so he got punishment too. She gripped the back of his head and pulled him to her breast. He unsnapped her bra in the back and pulled it smoothly from her arms, then sucked hard on her nipple. Holy hell she'd never wanted a man more than him. He knew exactly what she liked, knew exactly how to toe the line of pleasure and pain. His hand was rough on her one breast, massaging it as he paid attention to the other with his mouth. And then he sank to his knees suddenly and shoved her knees wider. Before she could balk, his mouth was on her sex, and his tongue was buried deep inside of her. She lost her damn mind. Gen could feel the vibration of her helpless moan in her chest, but didn't care what she sounded like right now. There was no more control as his head bobbed between her thighs, as he licked her until she shook, until her belly quivered and her legs went numb. Until he built the fire in her center so hot she threw her head back and let go completely. Orgasm shattered her, blasting through her body from where his tongue was thrusting into her upward. So intense, and she was gripping his hair in desperation. She could feel him growling against her sensitive clit as he sucked.

And then he was on her. He was up, shoving his jeans down his hips, then an arm around her back as he yanked her toward him. He wasn't gentle, and she didn't want him to be. Grey rammed into her, filling her. God, he was so big. Thick and long, and she had to remind herself to relax so she could take all of him. The second thrust, he pushed into her all the way. He entwined his fingers with hers and pulled her arm behind her back, pressed it against her spine to keep her completely at his mercy, and she fucking loved this. Loved him in control, loved him teaching her what he liked. Oh, outside of intimacy, he held doors for her, gave her tiny flowers, and carried her things. But in the bedroom, he liked to be boss. Sexy Greyson. He made a really good boss.

He bucked harder and harder, his powerful hips thrusting as he pulled her against him. Her boobs were smashed against his impossibly strong chest. His lips and teeth were all over her mouth and neck. She was coming again. Again, again, it was happening again. Greyson! Fuck, she wished she could hear. Wished she could hear to scream his name, and hear the sexy grunts in his throat as he pummeled her. Another orgasm took her, and with her free hand, she raked her nails down his back. He arched for her and slammed into her again, throbbing deep inside of her, filling her with bursts of warmth. His dick pulsed over and over, and then slower until he was spent. They moved together until both of their releases faded completely.

He turned gentle in a second. His lips went soft against hers like a quiet apology she didn't need because she adored the way he'd taken her. It was the sexiest experience she'd ever been a part of. His hands went gentle as he released her arm from her back and stroked her cheek. Kiss, kiss, soft kiss, soft lips. Soft sucks on her jaw, her earlobe, her neck. Soft touches as he ran his fingertips between her breasts, down, down to her sex. He eased his shaft out of her and pushed his fingers back into her, massaging her slowly, bringing the fire back as his mouth moved against hers. Again? Three? He wanted three orgasms from her? Felt so good. Gen grabbed the wrist of his hand resting on her cheek to keep him there. She craved his gentle touch after the chaos of their lovemaking. With her other hand, she cupped his where he was fingering her, showed him the pace she needed. Grey smiled against her lips, then eased out of her and put her own hand against her sex, and now he was the one setting the pace as he made her touch herself. Sexy, sexy, sexy. He eased out of the kiss and stared down between her legs as he helped her take care of herself. Oh, he liked watching her touch herself. Four more strokes and the pressure released, and she was softly pulsing around her fingers.

Greyson released her hand and put both arms around her, hugged her close to his body. He didn't leave to go clean up or try to get away from her. He just…held her for so long.

Gen's chest ached where it was pressed against his. It ached but felt oddly good and warm.

And inside, her gorilla whispered something life-changing.

He's mine. No matter what, he's mine.

ELEVEN

Crash! Shhhit, Greyson had been distracted all damn night and dropped another glass. Second one since his shift started.

"What's going on, man?" Jessie asked. The young bar owner had his dark eyebrows arched up in judgement. "Those glasses ain't free, and I thought you shifters were supposed to have magical reflexes. Where's your head at tonight, Grey?"

On Gen's wet little sex, on the taste of her, on watching her finger herself, on how she kissed, on how she'd bitten his neck almost hard enough for a claiming mark. On how she'd felt under his hands as he'd cleaned her in the shower. On his big plans to sleep with her in 1010 tonight just to wake up with her in his arms.

Gen took up every inch of his headspace right now. He needed to get it together. "I gotta girl," he admitted to Jessie.

"The girl? Because I have to tell you, the smile on your face is super stupid and mushy-looking right now."

Grey scratched the back of his head and ducked his gaze so he could hide the heat in his cheeks. "Yeah, the girl. I found her. It's new, so I'm kinda messed up about it."

"Damn," Jessie murmured, leaning on the bar. "Well, get it together, McCarty. We'll be busy tonight. Have you thought about my offer anymore? I need help. Jean's due with the baby any day now, and I can't be working as many shifts as I am. I need someone I can depend on. Preferably someone who stops breaking all my damn glasses."

Grey chuckled from where he was picking up the biggest shards and dropping them in the glass bucket. "I'm your guy. I need the money."

"Seriously? Yes?"

"Answer is hell yes. I appreciate the opportunity, Jessie." Because not that many people, human or shifter, gave chances to black-marked shifters like Grey. Jessie was young, three years younger than Grey was, but he was a fair boss.

"Great. Fuck yes to all of this. Jean is gonna be so happy. You start this week."

Grey nodded and swept the little glass shards into a dustpan. Spending nights away from Gen was going to suck balls, but he needed to man up for her. She wanted to hear, and he was going to bust his ass to make sure that happened for her.

"Whiskey and coke," a familiar voice growled out. Fucking Seth. Grey barely resisted the urge to take one of the big, jagged pieces of glass and jam it into the alpha of Cold Mountain's neck.

"What do you want?" Grey asked, standing up slowly.

"Trouble."

Seth's pride was standing behind him, chests puffed out, eyes gold like they were already halfway to a fight. He'd seen this game before, though. They didn't know the monster inside of him, didn't understand what his panther was, and they kept pushing him. They were lucky Grey had trained himself to be patient. There was no way in hell he was gonna end up in shifter prison like his dad. That's what everyone waited for, right? For him to be exactly like Dad. It's why he'd forced himself to be a quiet man, a patient hunter, to not react when assholes like these lions pushed too hard.

"No trouble here, sorry boys. We're out of whiskey and coke, too. You'll have to look elsewhere."

Seth leaned forward, the silver claw-mark scars on his face shining in the dim bar lighting. "You have until tomorrow to give us an answer."

"I can give you the answer now," Grey said, locking his arms against the bar top. "Fuck you. Your deal puts my crew at risk. I'm not doing it. I would rather cut my own leg off than go into business with a fucking lion pride." He jerked his chin toward the door. "Piss off."

Seth's face twisted up in fury, and he curled his lips back from teeth too long. He slammed his hand against the counter and gritted out, "You're gonna regret that decision, *panther*."

Probably, but he was in between a rock and a hard place, and he had to choose one. He chose Red Havoc, and Gen. And if the lions tried to retaliate, well, Grey would finally let his panther out. Nobody around here had really seen him, not even Ben. They'd seen the tamed-down, tightly-controlled version of Grey's animal.

Seth should let this go if he wanted to live.

"That guy's a dingleberry," Whiskey Barney slurred from the barstool he sat in. He was twisted around, watching the four lion shifters leave. "You should use that taser I got you for your birthday on them."

"Barney, you never gave me a taser," Grey said, shaking his head as he went back to washing the beer glasses.

"Yes, I did. I disting...dick-stinky..."

"Distinctly."

"Distinctly remember giving you a camo taser."

"That was me, Barney," Jessie said helpfully as he made drinks for a bachelorette party at the end of the bar. "You gave me a camo taser for Christmas, not my birthday."

"Oh." Whiskey Barney frowned and swung his unsteady gaze to Grey. "I'll get you one too, so you don't feel left out."

"You toting a taser here is a terrifying thought, WB."

"Plus, he's a panther," Jessie called helpfully. "He doesn't need weapons. He's got claws."

"You're a shifter?" Whiskey Barney asked in a high-pitched voice.

Grey snorted. "We've literally talked about this fourteen dozen times."

The door swung open, letting natural light in, and a familiar scent hit his nose—Gen's shampoo, body spray, her skin, and his sex on her. His dick throbbed immediately.

She offered him a beaming grin the second she saw him. She wore her short hair straight, bangs swept to the side, a red sparkly headband to match her red sequined tank top. Her black skinny jeans were shredded on the thighs, and she wore black high heels, also sparkly. She looked utterly beautiful and fuckable. Mine, mine, mine. Thank God, those lions had already left. If Gen was here to let loose, he wanted her to have fun, not worry about their glares on her.

Behind her, Jenny, Annalise, Kaylee, and Eden poured in the front door. Panther, panther, lioness, falcon, and his sexy gorilla was leading the girls' night charge. Good. Jenny had listened to him. He'd asked her to take Gen out and show her a good time. Get to know her. Because if Jenny fell for Gen, which was easy to do because his lady was incredible, she could change Ben's mind. So, Grey was being a dick by using Ben's mate to manipulate the alpha. He would go to insane lengths to keep Gen. This was kiddy-play.

Plus, bonus, Jenny had brought her here. He didn't have to spend the entire night imagining her. He could look at her.

Geez, this boner was ridiculous. Good thing the bar blocked his nethers from the customers because it was probably going to be a frequent occurrence tonight. Gen looked sexy as hell.

She strode up to the bar, eighty percent confidence, twenty percent flushed cheeks and ducking gaze. Not giving two shits what anyone thought about it, Grey leaned over the bar and pulled her into a kiss. A rough one that told her he was gonna fuck the shit out of her later. *Mine, mine, my sexy gorilla girl.* His chest was rattling with his panther's possessive growl, but he didn't care. Everyone here knew he was a shifter. Except Whiskey Barney, apparently, who sometimes forgot his own name and address.

When Gen bit his bottom lip gently, he just about lost it. It was a huge feat of self-control not to pull her over the bar, take her in the back, flip her around, splay her hands on the wall, smack that perfect ass, and drive into her from behind until his dick was throbbing inside of her. He wanted her to make more noises like she had earlier when they'd lost control with each other.

She did let off a little sigh that made his knees go to shit.

The girls were clapping and whistling, all but Jenny, who watched them through narrowed eyes. Screw hiding, though. The alpha's mate should know he was sinking his claws deep into his mate, and he wasn't letting Gen go. Not unless she wanted to be let go, which, from the way she swayed drunkenly against the bar when he told her how sexy she looked tonight, Gen didn't feel like going anywhere.

When her lightened, silver eyes went to his lips, he smiled and asked, "Girls' night?"

She nodded and signed something fast. Something long. Her hands were graceful as she worked. He shook his head. "I don't understand. Not yet." But he would, because he was going to learn how to speak her language as fast as possible.

Gen looked stunned, and then embarrassed, as if she'd forgotten they couldn't communicate like that. Grey was feeling pa-retty fuckin' cocky about his kiss now. He'd shorted out her circuits, like she did to him.

Gen pulled her phone out and typed away while Grey nodded to the girls gathering at the bar. "What are you all drinking tonight?"

"Everything!" Annalise said excitedly.

"She started pre-drinking at home," Kaylee explained through a giggle.

Grey laughed and said, "How about I start you off with some panty droppers. Girl shots? I can make them pink and sweet. Unlike you little cretins."

The girls looked eerily similar with the strange grins they all wore.

"What?" he asked as his phone chirped with Gen's message.

"You're different tonight, Ghost Cat," Jenny murmured.

Grey made a tick sound and checked his phone. That nickname didn't bother him. He liked being invisible. Gen had said, *Jenny and the girls invited me out. I haven't been to a bar in years. I don't even know what I like to drink, but I'm so excited they want to hang out with me! I already knew Eden, but the other girls are way nicer than the females in the family group. I like you and your butt.* There were three flame emojis that followed and then a 8---D.

Grey laughed at her hand-made dick emoji and typed back, *You look sexy as hell and this is happening the second we're alone 8---D (0)*

"See!" Kaylee said as he began making their shots. "You're smiling. It looks weird on you."

"Thanks a lot," Grey muttered.

"You feel different, too," Jenny said, eyes narrowed to suspicious little slits. "You feel…not like a grumpy demon."

"Her fault," Grey said, jerking his chin at Gen.

She looked confused, but after Eden signed something to her, she nodded and smiled, her cheeks going all pink again. *Mine.*

He lined up their shots and made them pink and sweet like Gen's little p-word, and when she reached for hers, he caught her attention. "Have fun tonight, okay? Cut loose, forget about everything, dance, laugh out loud. Just don't dance with Whiskey Barney," he said, pointing to the man grinning at them. "He's a handsy pervert on the dance floor." He gave her a wink as Whiskey Barney complained about Grey being a clock-blocker, which he probably meant to say cock-blocker, but it was eleven o'clock and WB was five shots in.

Gen grinned so big, so pretty, and then she turned and raised her little shot glass with the other girls. Eden did the toast, but time and time again, Gen's big blue eyes landed on Grey. Fuck it. It was too soon, but he loved her. He loved her with a scary intensity. His cat had known she was his from early on. Every smile she gave made his heart stop. It made him desperate to make her smile again, and that's what love was…right? It was someone else's happiness coming before all else.

And for the next few hours, he watched his favorite girl smile, laugh, and bond with the females of the Red Havoc Crew. Oh, the girls were tough. They were strong, dominant, and not afraid to fight for the people they loved, and Gen, even as a submissive, not able to hear, was hanging with them. He was so damn proud. And if he was honest, he had really wanted the girls' approval for her. He wanted Gen to fit in, and he wanted the girls to like her. They danced together, cut up, drank…

Gen figured out she liked pickle-back shots— shots of vodka with pickle juice chasers. He bought all the drinks so the girls didn't have to worry about anything, just have fun. And when Jenny started drinking water to sober up, he told her he would take them all home, so Jenny could just cut loose with the others.

"Really?"

"Yep, really. I'll get your truck in the morning. Go have fun with the girls."

Jenny looked all emotional. "It's just…I'm a mom and a wife and mate to the alpha, and I'm supposed to be perfect—"

"Fuck that. You don't have to be perfect. No one else in Red Havoc is. Be you. You're a great mom, an awesome mate for Ben. You can have fun, and it won't make us look differently at you."

Jenny was crying now. Woman tears were terrifying, but Grey stood his ground and handed her a bar napkin. With a loud sniff, she dabbed her done-up eyes and gave him a trembling smile. "In that case,

I'll have another one of those panty-droppers."

"Thata girl," he said, pulling the vanilla vodka and watermelon schnapps. The bachelorette party at the end of the bar was tossing these things back like water, so he was a pro at making them now.

Whiskey Barney leaned forward and pointed to it. "Can I have one of—"

"No, you're cut off."

"Asstroll." He probably meant asshole.

Jenny snorted, but finally she'd stopped crying, thank God. He handed her the drink, but Jenny shocked him to his core when she grabbed his wrist and looked him dead in the eyes. She twitched her shoulder-length brunette hair away from her face and murmured, "You know Ben banishing Gen isn't about her, right?"

Grey shook his head slowly. "What's it about then?"

Her delicate little throat moved as she swallowed hard. "It's about you, Grey. About what you're fighting. About what you're supposed to be."

Maybe Jenny was drunker than he'd thought. "I don't understand."

"He knows what you are." Jenny cocked one dark

eyebrow, slammed her shot, set down the glass, and walked to the dancefloor to join the girls without looking back at him.

Grey sighed. Well, shit. If Ben knew what he'd been hiding all this time…it complicated things.

Now it would be even harder to get Gen into Red Havoc.

TWELVE

Unable to help herself, Gen snuck a glance at Grey for the hundredth time in two hours. He'd been distracted all night. Not just with work either. Sure, he stayed busy, but it was more than that. Half the time she looked over at him, he'd been staring at her, too. But the other half, he'd looked troubled, his blond brows lowered, and his eyes not quite their blue human color. It had happened after Jenny talked to him. Maybe she'd told him Gen really couldn't get into the crew.

That felt right. Gen's heart sank. Today had been the best day in as long as she could remember, first with Grey and then with the girls' night. If she was cast out into the world again, she would always think of this as the life-that-got-away.

She excused herself from the table where the girls were talking and laughing and made her way through the empty room to where Grey was counting money behind the bar.

"I'm trying to hurry," he said, enunciating so well for her. He always did. Sensitive and caring mate.

It's okay, she mouthed. He shoved the money into a blue bank bag and stuck the yellow wooden pencil he'd been using behind his ear. As he turned toward the register, she caught his hand. *Are you okay?*

His smile was too bright, too quick a response, and too empty. "I'm great."

I'm really not allowed in the crew?

The fake smile disappeared, and there it was, frustration in his eyes. "I'm gonna take care of it."

Can I do anything?

He shook his head and drew her knuckles to his lips. His kiss lingered there for a three-count before he said, "Not this time." Grey leaned toward her, resting his elbows on the bar top. "You didn't wash my scent off you from when we were together earlier."

On purpose. I like smelling like you.

Now his smile was genuine. Genuinely wicked. He twitched his head toward a hallway. "You wanna see the office?"

Her eyes were probably the size of twin moons as she checked over her shoulder at the girls at the table on the other side of the bar. They were pigging out on wings and sweet potato fries and were laughing about something. She wished she could hear them.

When she looked back at Grey, he said, "I'll have you so fast, they won't even miss us."

Okay then. Gen hustled to the hallway and followed Grey past the bathrooms to an office in the back. He shut the door behind them and thank goodness someone had left a little desk lamp on, because Grey didn't bother to turn on the main light. He just rounded on her and slid his arms around her waist, lifted her off the floor so she could wrap her legs around him. And then he walked them to the wall until her back was pressed hard against it. Grey rocked his erection into her, and even through her jeans, he hit her perfectly.

They didn't have time for fooling around or the girls really would miss them, so Gen pulled at his shirt with desperate, shaking fingers. Grey only stopped kissing her long enough to set her down and push her pants down her legs, but then she was back up, legs wrapped around his hips, his mouth urgent on hers again. He didn't prepare her, but she didn't need it. She'd been turned on all night watching him manage the bar and order everyone around. He was so confident, so sure of himself. He was powerful even if he pretended he wasn't. Even if he chose to be the bottom of his crew.

Grey slid into her by a few inches, withdrew, and then bucked his hips and slammed deep inside her. She made a sound in her throat at how good he felt inside of her but didn't give a single care right now. He held her tightly and pumped into her so deep, and so fast, she was already on the edge. With one hand, she held onto the back of his neck for balance, and with the other, she gripped the back of his hair. Harder and harder he pounded her until the pressure was blinding. So good. This felt *soooo* good. His teeth went to her neck, and she shattered, pulsing around his shaft. Grey slammed into her deep and joined her release. His dick throbbed inside her with every slow pump of his hips, and that strange and sexy rattling sensation was back, vibrating from his chest to hers.

Their heartbeats raced each other, and their breaths came ragged, and when Grey eased back, he was smiling so big his teeth showed white in the dim lamplight. He looked like a proud rooster, and it made her giggle. She could tell it made a sound though from the feel of it in her throat, and she got self-conscious and looked away.

Grey's finger was gentle on her jaw as he pulled her attention back to him. "I. Love. Your. Laugh."

Gen dragged her knuckles against his blond beard and tested a voice she couldn't hear. "I. Love. You."

Grey inhaled sharply and shook his head, looking at her with an expression that said she was beautiful. Like she was the moon and the stars. She'd never witnessed a dominant man like him look so emotional. He kissed her lips, her nose, each of her cheeks, then her forehead.

And when he eased back, his lips formed the most important words she'd ever seen. "I. Love. You. Too."

THIRTEEN

Grey inhaled deeply and stretched behind her. She'd always been a light sleeper, so any movement he made in the night, she had adjusted with him. He'd dropped the girls off but had asked her to stay in his bed tonight. He hadn't even tried anything with her, just held her as they fell asleep. Even now, in the silver light before dawn, he pulled her closer against his torso.

His chest vibrated with his words, and Gen forced her eyes open so she could read his lips.

"I'll be back in a little while. Get some more sleep, Gen. I'll bring back breakfast."

He wasn't smiling though, and his eyes were tight. Something was wrong.

Desperate to stall him leaving, she mouthed slowly, *Why did Jenny call you Ghost Cat last night?*

He frowned and dragged a light touch along the edge of her earlobe. "Because I keep to myself. I stay as invisible as I can. I'm at home in the shadows."

It didn't seem to bother him, but she didn't like that nickname. Grey wasn't a ghost. He was a good man. She saw him just fine.

Grey let his lips linger against her forehead and hugged her close. She held on too, pressed against his naked body under the sheets because she didn't understand why he was worked up, why his eyes were gold, or the rattle in his chest was constant. She pressed her palm against his pec to see if she could settle the sound there, but it vibrated on. There was a lot in Grey's life that she couldn't fix, or even improve, and she hated it. The man carried so much more of the world on his shoulders than he admitted. He'd been hiding how he protected the Red Havoc Crew, hiding his run-ins with the lions. And now he was staring out the window in the dim light before dawn with trouble brewing in every facet of his face. He was stroking her hair, running his fingers through it, but his eyes were dead.

Greyson looked like he was preparing for war.

He nipped at her neck and then rolled out of bed. His back was to her as he dressed, and then he disappeared into the bathroom to come back a few minutes later smelling of mint toothpaste when he leaned down and kissed her. "Sleep."

She tried to hold onto his hand, but he let his fingertips slip out of hers and left the room. A few seconds later, the vibration of the front door shutting brushed her skin. Frowning, Gen got up, wrapped the sheet around her, and padded toward the window. It was barely light outside, but illuminated enough she could see Grey walk toward his waiting alpha. Ben looked somber as he watched Greyson approach. They talked for a minute, but she couldn't read their lips from here.

And then Grey and Ben removed their clothes and their panthers ripped out of them like magic.

Within the span of a quick breath, they were fighting like they wanted to kill each other.

It made her sick to watch them slapping, clawing, biting. Her inner gorilla wanted to explode out of her skin and help Grey, but he'd said that wouldn't fix it. It would only drag out whatever he and Ben were trying to work out. The fight seemed to last for hours, but it was probably a minute, perhaps two, tops. Grey disengaged and slunk into the woods, black fur matted and wet, long claw marks down his shoulder, his ears flat as he disappeared like a phantom into Red Havoc Woods.

He wouldn't want her seeing him hurt, so she stayed right where she was, watching out the window for her panther to return. All the while, she felt sick. This wasn't how it was supposed to be. Grey should be in bed with her, not being bled by his alpha. This was her fault. Ben was hurting him because she wasn't leaving, but what were her options? Leave Grey? That felt impossible now. Stay? That also felt impossible when Grey was off in those woods bleeding somewhere.

Be brave?

She'd been fucking brave and chosen the life she wanted…and now it was hurting the man she loved.

FOURTEEN

One week.

Torren had said he would call in one week, but he hadn't. Gen had checked her phone a hundred times today, and no call, no message, no nothing. Shit, shit, shit.

She tried calling him again, but it went straight to voicemail, just like every other time. Something had gone wrong.

If something bad happened to Torren...

God, she couldn't even think like that. Couldn't imagine life without her big brother. He'd been there to protect her for always. They'd grown up having each other's backs because they'd been raised right outside of Damon's Mountains. She'd relied on

Torren growing up. He was her brother, but also her best friend.

She wanted to talk to someone, share the burden, but Grey had been pulling away over the last couple of days. It was Ben's fault. Gen wrung her hands as she sat on the steps of 1010 and stared out at the daisy field. Many of the little white flowers were painted with crimson now. Every morning, at the same time, Ben waited for Grey out in this field, and Grey met him, every day. And every day, she watched her mate be punished for her being here. She watched him bleed. She watched him hold back and pull out of the fight without hurting Ben. Something bad was happening to him though, on the insides. Grey's smile didn't come as easy, and he hurt. He wasn't healing as fast. He was hiding injuries from her, but she saw everything. She watched him undress after he worked at the bar every night, traced the claw marks on his back and arms and chest. She winced at the teeth marks that had ruined the skin of his neck. Not even his tattoos could hide the scars now.

Every time she asked him if she should leave, he would get angry and hold her so tightly. And then he would beg her not to go. "Never go. Don't leave me, or I can't do this." But "this" was a concept she didn't understand, and he wouldn't explain.

Gen had told herself to wait the week, and if Torren took care of any danger Sean posed, then she would go to Ben again, tell him she was safe for the crew, and he could stop punishing Grey. She really, really needed the punishment to stop because, inside of her, the gorilla wanted to rip Ben apart limb-by-limb. She hadn't Changed all week just to make sure she could keep in control around him.

The crew was sitting around a fire pit in front of Ben and Jenny's cabin, talking. Twice, Eden had waved her over, but Gen had ignored them. They were good at including her—amazing, actually—but she'd seen herself in the mirror. Silver eyes that wouldn't turn human blue anymore because the gorilla wanted out of her skin so badly. Red Havoc was full of dominant monsters, and she could trigger their Changes too, if she wasn't careful. Plus, she was waiting for Grey to get back from moonshine deliveries.

Gen checked her phone again. Nothing. Fuck. *Torren, where are you?*

The fine hairs on her arms rose, and she felt watched. When she arched her gaze back to the bonfire, Ben was staring at her with a calculating look in his blue eyes. Gen barely resisted the urge to flip him off before she gave her attention back to the bloody daisies.

The sun was setting behind her, behind the mountains that surrounded Red Havoc Territory, and it made the shadows of the trees long. It saturated everything in gray light. Gray. Grey. Grey was light.

Just the thought of leaving him felt like a knife in the heart, but she couldn't watch him bleed every day because of her. That's not what love was. It wasn't hurting the person who meant everything just so she could be comfortable and stay here.

Grey's truck bumped slowly up the dirt road toward her. He parked by her Mustang, a tight smile for her on his lips. But the second he looked over at the bonfire, his eyes went dead again. Ben was standing now, removing his shirt, eyes locked on Greyson.

No, no, no, it wasn't morning yet, and they'd just fought twelve hours ago. Grey wouldn't be healed enough for this.

He shoved the door open and spat on the ground. When he cast her a quick glance, his eyes were vivid gold and his face was twisted in a feral mask of fury. Gen stood and bolted for him, then stood in front of him as he walked, pushing against his chest.

"Stop it, Gen." He tried to avoid her, but she stuck on him like glitter on glue because this was messed up. It was more than she could take, more than she could bear.

Desperately, she looked to Eden and Jaxon for help, and thank God, Jax was headed her way. But when he reached them, he pulled Gen off Grey by the waist.

She fought viciously, kicking his shins, but his grip on her only tightened, and now Grey was almost to Ben in the field of bloody flowers. "No!" she screamed loud, the words scratching up her throat. She didn't care if it was off-key or thick-sounding. She didn't care about anything but saving Grey. His arm under his sleeve was mauled still from the fight this morning. "Noooo," she screamed again, struggling as Jax and Eden and Barret now held her. The gorilla was here, ready. She was going to kill Ben. Kill. Ben. Kill him. Protect Grey.

Eden stood in front of her, so Gen craned her neck, trying to see around her. Get the fuck out of the way!

Eden was signing something, her eyes serious. Signing something...fast...in simple alphabet. *Ben is trying to help.*

Jax released Gen's arms, but not her waist.

"Fuck Ben," Gen yelled.

No, not fuck Ben, Eden was mouthing the words with her sign language now. *Grey is supposed to be alpha!*

Gen stared at her, completely shocked to stillness. "What?" she signed.

"Can't you feel him, Gen? Can't you feel the cat inside of him? He tried to hide it, but he can't hide from Ben. Ben isn't the most dominant panther here. He's pushing him because he has to, Gen. And you have to let him do it. Balance has to be restored to Red Havoc. You brought out Grey's protective instincts, his dominance. There's no more hiding for him."

Grey and Ben were talking now, shirts off, chests puffed up. They both looked pissed. Oh God, they'd been fighting alpha fights? Ben didn't understand!

Gen turned on Jax and let her gorilla out enough to roar in his face. Smart man let her go, and she bolted for Grey. Before she reached him though, Ben held out his hand. "Stop. Gen, this needs to happen."

"Why?" she asked out loud. Fuck what she sounded like. "Why!" she screamed.

It was Grey who answered, enunciating his words carefully. "Ben thinks I want alpha."

Ben's face turned beet red. "No! I think you *need* it. I can't run this crew when no one listens to my orders. I couldn't figure out why everyone was disobeying my orders all the fucking time, and then it hit me the day Gen showed up, the day you let your guard down, and I felt your monster! The crew isn't minding me because there is another contender for alpha." Ben jammed his finger against Grey's chest. "You."

Gen was crying tears of anger, but screw everything. She signed simply to Grey, *I thought you were being punished because of me.*

Grey hugged her so fast, so hard, it stole her breath away. He gripped her hair in the back and made her look at his face. "Ben's trying to get me to fight. He used kicking you out of the territory to get me riled up. I don't want alpha. I don't want to fight. I'm stuck. I'm not my father. I don't need power. Don't want it. I want bottom of the crew. My dad reached for Alpha, and look where he is? And look where that hunger for power got me! Banished from my crew. I just want to be invisible." Grey looked sick as he searched her eyes for understanding. "I just want to be invisible with you."

Gen clutched his arms and sobbed because, God, she hadn't known he was fighting this war alone. He hadn't reached his potential, and now Ben was trying to push him to it. But the more Grey fought being like his father, the more he got hurt. And suddenly, it hit her. She'd hated Ben this week. Hated him for hurting her mate, hated him for being a bad alpha. But he wasn't being a bad alpha. He was trying to help. Trying to restore the balance of his crew, even if that meant giving up his place as king of these mountains.

Ben was trying to get Grey to rise up and fight for his throne.

I just want to be invisible with you.

"Grey," she said, hoping to God her words sounded okay. "You. Aren't. A. Ghost."

Her phone vibrated in her back pocket.

She ignored it because Grey had her trapped in his gaze. He rested his hands on his hips and snarled up his lip, shaking his head. Ben was moving toward her mate, but she couldn't take her eyes off Grey's churning, golden eyes.

Her phone vibrated again and again, back-to-back. Grey was yelling at Ben now, the veins standing out in his neck as he unbuttoned his jeans. He didn't want to do this, but what choice did he have? Balance was pivotal to a crew staying intact. His panther was hurting the dynamics here by not taking his place in the ranking of dominance.

Her phone vibrated again. Gen yanked it out of her back pocket and sighed in relief when she saw Torren's name on the caller ID. But the weight slammed back down onto her shoulders the second she read his messages.

Gen I was wrong

The Crew of Two Wars

The first one is yours

Get inside!!!! Get everyone inside. Help is coming.

What? Terrified, she scanned the woods, but they'd gone eerily still. They'd turned scary as the final rays of daylight struggled to reach deeper into the forest.

When a massive shadow moved across the tree line, Gen patted the air, utterly stunned by the terror that filled her chest, but trying to get the boys' attention. "Grey," she said, forcing air past her vocal cords to a whisper.

The shadow in the woods came closer. Her heart banged against her ribcage when she laid eyes on the enormous, blue-eyed silverback who had taken everything from her—her pride, her money, her chance at hearing. She'd run for good reason, but he was here for her. Torren hadn't been able to stop Beaston's Crew of Two Wars prophesy.

"Grey," she repeated, wishing so badly she could hear what he and the alpha were yelling, but their lips moved too fast for her to read, and now they were circling each other. Gen was frozen in panic as Sean charged, his meaty knuckles punching the earth with each stride, his eyes filled with rage. His deadly gaze was on Grey. Oh, God. He knew she had paired up, and he was in this for a kill. It was the gorillas' way. He would have Grey's exposed neck snapped like a twig before Grey even knew he was in danger.

Behind the charging silverback, the trees shook

with shadows, limbs snapping, hitting the ground, leaves raining as the females from her family group screamed and bore their long teeth. And like Sean had given them a signal, all of them, all thirty females, hit the ground and were charging, too.

Grey was too far away and focused, so was Ben. All she could do was protect her mate from the first wave of destruction—Sean.

Rage boiled her blood, and all she saw was red. He'd taken enough. She would be damned if he took Grey away from her, too. With a roar of fury, she let the gorilla have her body. Fuck being submissive. Fuck being half Sean's weight. Fuck the little voice inside her head that used to say she wasn't good enough, wasn't strong enough, that she couldn't do this. She killed that voice the second her knuckles hit the blood-stained flowers. Lips curled back so Sean could see what was coming for his throat, she charged him, cut off his line of sight to Grey. His focus shifted to her, but she wasn't backing down, she wasn't slowing down, and she sure as shit wasn't playing chicken tonight.

My mate.

My crew.

My territory.

My war.

Sean was gonna paint the flowers red tonight for coming here and threatening the life she wanted. For threatening the people she loved. At the last moment, she pushed off her back legs and leapt through the air. She slammed into Sean with the force of two eighteen-wheelers colliding. She could feel the wave of power from that collision blast through her body, but she didn't feel the pain. Maybe it was the adrenaline, but she didn't feel anything as she pummeled her fists against his face. He was off balance as they hit the ground. She sank her teeth deep into his shoulder just as he wrapped his giant hand around her arm. Sean threw her hard, but she dragged her canines through his muscle, inflicting as much damage as she could before she was flung sideways and skidded through the dirt. Grey was on the silverback before he had any time to recover.

In the span of a breath, the clearing had erupted in chaos. Jaxon's massive grizzly was tearing through two gorillas, Annalise's She-Devil had her claws sunk deep into the back of another. Eden's albino falcon was ripping her talons at the face of Margo, Sean's favorite female. Kaylee's lioness had another by the leg, preventing her from running. Ben, Barret, Anson, all of them had Changed in a moment and were brawling. She was so fucking proud. Gorillas were huge and with bone-crushing strength, but her crew wasn't backing down.

It wouldn't be enough, though.

Thirty gorillas meant certain death for every one of the Red Havoc Crew. They were buying time, that's all. Their breaths were numbered because gorillas trained for war. Secret wars between each other. Wars over females. Entire family groups annihilating each other for territory. They lived to kill.

Grey was the only one fighting Sean, and she couldn't get to him. *Can't get to him. Can't.* The female she battled was named Merin. She was one who helped to break her, but Gen wasn't the same weak submissive she'd been before. She'd spent too much time with the badasses of Red Havoc, and now her gorilla was too angry at this war to let up on Merin. She beat her powerful fists against her and yanked her leg out from under her. Merin was vicious with her fists, and Gen was running out of time. She needed to help Grey. Every instinct in her said to stay close to him, so she hit Merin so hard her arm rattled with the force, and then she bolted for Sean. Grey was latched onto the back of his neck, but he was about to be thrown against a tree. It was Sean's move, but she could stop it if she was fast enough.

The force of impact with the silverback forced the air from her lungs in a huff. He threw Grey, but messed it up. It was a desperation move to save his throat, and rushed, and she'd hit Sean right as the silverback had grabbed Grey's leg, so he didn't go far. He landed on his feet, and then he was bolting for her again. She fought like some wild, injured creature, pummeling Sean with her fists.

Fuck him for telling her she was nothing.

She was the daughter of Kong.

She was mate to the Ghost Cat.

Whether Ben liked it or not, she was going to die *as* Red Havoc *with* Red Havoc. This was the crew of her heart.

Something inside of her broke at the thought of this being the end. It wasn't fair. She hadn't lived this life long enough. She'd only just found Grey and her crew. She'd only just found happiness.

She was hurting now. The numbness was gone.

Sean was ruthless. His teeth sank into her bicep, and there were hands ripping at her. Sean's females were rallying, protecting him. Where was Grey? She couldn't see him through the hoard of massive bodies.

Sean slammed her to the ground under him so hard her breath whooshed out of her lungs, and she couldn't draw it again. He slammed his fists against the ground on either side of her face and roared, exposing three-inch canines. This was it—the end. His blazing blue eyes dipped to her throat, and all she could do with his massive weight on top of her was cover her face as he pierced her skin right at the base of her neck.

But in an instant, the pain disappeared along with his weight, and shocked, Gen looked up to see Torren's monstrous gorilla stand up on his hind legs, blazing green eyes on Sean as he beat his chest and roared in challenge. Sean was slow to get up off the ground where he'd been tackled.

He'd come. Torren had come for Red Havoc. For her. He'd ripped Sean away from her just in time. Dad would be so fucking proud if he saw Torren slamming into Sean to defend her right now. Panting, she looked around, but Grey had pulled the females off her and was in trouble. Everyone was in trouble. The crew was losing their battles now, playing defense, protecting themselves. Furious, Gen charged the females, prepared to fight to her last breath if it meant helping Grey. He had to exist on this earth, or what was the point of anything?

As she hit the gorillas, a great wind hit the clearing so hard, Gen was slammed to the ground. When she caught her breath again and looked up, a terrifying beast blocked out the entire sky.

Torren had said help was on the way, but she hadn't expected this.

He'd called in Destruction.

He'd called in Death.

He'd called in his best friend, the mother-fucking red dragon.

He'd called in Vyr, son of Damon and Clara Daye.

The dragon pulled a tight circle and showed his blood-red belly scales and black claws. And with a roar that shook the earth beneath her, Vyr opened his mouth, exposing hundreds of razor sharp teeth. And then he spewed a line of fire across the clearing, cutting off four females charging Jaxon and Annalise.

Heat blasted against Gen's face, and on instinct, she threw off the gorilla Grey was fighting and shoved him toward the woods. They needed to get clear of the dragon's wrath. This was why Torren had told her to get everyone inside. Vyr wasn't his father. He wasn't careful. He was fury and fire, fueled by protective instincts so strong they made him lose his reason and become reckless in battle.

Run. Run, run, run, Red Havoc, because Vyr was going to burn this territory to the ground.

Next to her, Grey was running with graceful, powerful strides. Beside him were Anson, Ben, Jax, the girls, and Barret. On her other side, Torren was running on all fours, twice her size, a fully mature silverback, attention on her. She'd never seen her brother scared, but fear dwelled in his bright green eyes and the set of his mouth.

Through the smoke, Jenny was up ahead with Raif and Bentley, screaming and waving them toward her. Her lips formed the words, "Hurry!"

Heat blistered Gen's back and urged her faster. Vyr roared again. She couldn't hear it, but she could feel the earth shaking with it. She'd always been afraid of the red dragon. Everyone was except for

Torren.

At the break in the heat, Gen skidded to a stop and spun around. Red Havoc woods were burning, and the surviving gorillas were scattering, bolting across the forest floor and swinging through the trees as fast as they could. Vyr dipped down, jaws open as he scooped ashes into his mouth. Arching his back and beating his massive crimson wings, he lifted into the sky and circled back.

Chest heaving, Gen looked at the line of her friends and her brother, standing there beside her, staring just like she had been at the red dragon as he fed. Silverback, lioness, panthers, falcon, grizzly—all covered in soot and blood. Jenny's eyes looked haunted as she hugged Raif and Bentley close against her legs and watched Vyr make another pass at the ashes he'd created.

Grey looked over at her, his gold eyes full of question. *Are you okay?*

Panting and in complete shock, Gen nodded slowly.

Beaston had called Red Havoc the Crew of Two Wars.

Well…they'd just survived the first.

FIFTEEN

I don't think I want you to watch, Grey signed. *I think I want to do it alone.*

Why alone? Gen signed back.

Grey frowned and stumbled on the explanation. His signs were clumsy, and they weren't word-for-word, but she seemed to get the gist. *I remember the day my dad killed the alpha in our crew. I remember the horror on the humans' faces. I'll challenge Ben, but I don't want you to look at me like that. Like the humans looked at my dad. At me. Like we were monsters.*

The early-morning breeze lifted the ends of her short hair, and she snuggled closer to Grey's side on the stairs to 1010. He loved her so much it scared him sometimes. She smelled like sleep and fruit shampoo and his Gen. Her signs were much more graceful than his, and thankfully she used the alphabet slowly so he could keep up. *Tonight, I'm going to move my stuff into your cabin. It doesn't matter if you are Alpha, or if you stay at the bottom of the crew. I'm going to move in with you either way. What you are doesn't matter to me. Who you are does.*

Sweet mate, settling the panther inside of him with just a few gestures. People said 1010 was magic, but it was Gen. She was the one who had come into his life and changed everything for the better. She was the best kind of magic. He kissed her temple and cupped her cheeks, and inside, his panther purred when she nuzzled his hand. Affectionate little gorilla. It was as if she'd been made just for him. As if they'd both had to go through struggles so they could appreciate each other fully. He was probably fucking this up, but he signed as best he could, *You said I wasn't a ghost. The other day, you said the words out loud, and I loved the sound of your voice as you said that.*

She blushed and tucked her chin to her chest. *I see you just fine.*

Heaving a sigh, Grey looked over at the crew, who were gathering around Ben in the field of charred daisies. He'd become so comfortable at hiding over the years. So good at being quiet. So good at invisibility. He'd trained his panther to pretend he was something he wasn't, but he'd gotten careless. He'd worked so hard not to be like Dad, and Ben was going to push him to fight. To really fight. To lose control. *Now everyone will see me.*

Gen signed slowly. *You won't kill Ben. I know you won't. You're scared of being like your dad, but you aren't. You have more self-control than any man I've ever met. Last fight with Ben over alpha. Win or lose, I'll be waiting to hug you up. Get it done, and we can come back to 1010 and get lost in our bed for a while. Fall back asleep. Move my stuff to your cabin. Last fight, and then we can get back to living.*

Grey drew her hand to his lips, kissed them in silent thank you, then pulled her up with him. "No more being invisible. No more Ghost Cat."

Gen looked so proud as she walked beside him. She'd been so strong in the war with the gorillas. So protective. Perfect. Three days ago, this place had been burned by dragon's fire in a battle that had showed him just how dedicated she was to him and this crew. She hadn't run. She'd been in the thick of it, right in the fray, fighting to the death. And truly, if Vyr and Torren hadn't showed up, it could've been to the death.

Brave mate. So fucking brave.

Inside, his panther was snarling, and restless with bloodlust. He was ready to bleed Ben. He'd been kept in check too much as time and time again Grey had left the fight early, just when he was hitting his stride. Why? Because he hadn't wanted to be alpha. He wouldn't be any good at it.

He pulled off his shirt and let it slip to the ground as he faced off with Ben. He expected the same fight as every other morning Ben had pushed him for a challenge. But today, Ben left his shirt on, and his eyes stayed blue. Ben's panther didn't burst out of him and bleed Grey like he thought would happen. No, instead, the alpha stepped forward and shocked Grey to his bones as he hugged him tightly and clapped him on the back. "You're ready now. I can feel it, and I know what you're capable of. I have for a while."

Ben dropped suddenly to his knees in the ashes

and exposed his neck. "I'm tired. Tired of fighting to hold a crew that isn't really mine to hold. Tired of all the big decisions resting on my shoulders. Tired of staying up nights wondering if I'm good enough to keep you all safe. That's your burden now."

"I don't understand," Grey murmured as Gen slipped her arm around his and held it tightly.

"If you didn't want anything to do with being alpha, you would've left, Grey. You would've taken Gen and gone. But you're still here."

"And still a motherfuckin' monster," Barret said unhelpfully.

"I want donuts," Anson complained. "Seriously, can your first alpha decision be to hurry this up so we can get breakfast?"

"I'm going to be super shitty at this," Grey admitted.

"Grey, you've been doing alpha stuff quietly for years," Ben said. "I know you've been watching our backs with the Cold Mountain Pride. I know you've protected us from other battles too, and never for attention like those assholes would do." Ben gestured to Anson and Barret.

"I resemble that," Barret muttered, chewing on

his thumbnail.

"Donuts," Anson reminded him.

God, this was a crew of idiots and C-Teamers, and Grey was really going to be the king of them.

Jenny made her way to Ben and knelt beside him with little Raif tucked against her. "You won't suck at this, Grey. You were built for this. You'll keep the crew steady. They'll listen to your orders and not question everything."

Jaxon raised his hand like a schoolboy. "I'll question everything." Annalise snorted and knelt in the ashes, then tugged Jax's jeans and pointed to the ground beside her. With a put-upon sigh, Jax lowered himself too and exposed his neck. "Try not to get us all killed."

One by one, the others dropped down until, beside him, Gen went to her knees last of all. She smiled up at him, looking so damn pretty with the dawn light touching her cheeks and her crystal blue eyes locked on him like he hung the moon.

He was going to do everything in his power to give her a safe home, and a safe crew.

With a sigh, he said, "First act as alpha... Genevieve Taylor, welcome to Red Havoc."

Her face transformed into a radiant smile, and her eyes rimmed with tears. Not the terrifying kind, but the kind that made his heart hold onto her a little bit tighter.

She stood so fast and jumped up into his arms with such force, he had to take a couple steps back to keep his balance. She left smacking kisses all over his face and made soft noises in her throat she probably didn't even know she was making, but were so fucking cute.

"Ew." Anson crossed his arms over his chest and scowled. "Okay, what's your second act as alpha?"

Grey set his mate on her feet and murmured, "Fine. Second act is breakfast."

"I'm driving!" Jaxon and Barret both yelled at the same time. "Jinx! Jinx again! Twins! Jinx, jinx, jinx. Pinch, poke, you owe me a coke." They'd said it all in unison and were now speed-walk-racing toward their trucks. And then they were jogging. Barret tripped Jaxon, and the grizzly shifter pitched forward and caught Barret's ankle on the way down. Barret fell on his face, and now they were wrestling in the ashes. The rest of the crew stepped around them, talking quietly amongst themselves like there weren't two grown-ass men rolling around and punching at each other's dicks.

God, his crew was weird. Grey gave a private smile. He secretly loved them.

Are you happy? Gen signed beside him.

Grey pulled her close against his ribs and kissed her soundly. Was he happy? Being alpha was going to be a huge pain in the ass, but he didn't have to hide what his panther was capable of anymore. He wouldn't have to dwell in the shadows. Everything had changed for the crew in a matter of weeks. Lynn was with the Gray Backs, trying to get better, Red Havoc Woods had been burnt to a crisp by a dragon, they'd survived a war, and now he was alpha. And for some reason, Ben looked relieved. He was smiling down at Jenny and Raif easier than Grey had seen him do in a long time.

On top of all that, Grey found his person. That was the best part—Gen. She was everything he ever could've imagined in his other half. She pushed him to be better, and stronger. To reach his potential. And he was the luckiest SOB on the planet to get to watch her grow stronger in the crew. He was so proud that she was his. There was no doubt in his mind that on the hard days of being alpha, she would be there, lending support and keeping him upright.

She didn't even know how incredible she was.

With her eyes glued to his lips, he admitted something he used to think would never be true for a man like him. "Yeah, Gen, I'm really happy."

SIXTEEN

Gen stood in front of Grey's dresser, untangling her necklaces from her earrings. She'd packed in a hurry when she'd left Sean and the family group ten days ago, and the tiny silver chains were all knotted around her other baubles.

Ten days, but it felt like so much longer because she'd changed so much in that short amount of time.

Movement caught her attention in the mirror, and she looked up to find Grey leaned up against the doorframe, watching her with a soft look in his eyes, as though he thought she was beautiful. He was the beautiful one though—Alpha. Caring, dominant, smart, protective, hard-working Red Havoc Guardian, he was everything she could ever hope for in a mate.

He was everything she could hope for in a best friend.

I have a surprise for you, he signed.

She turned with a ready grin because she already knew what it was. He gave her an oxeye daisy every day. It was sweet because the entire field had been burned by Vyr, so Grey went out and hunted down the little white flowers for her.

But Grey's hand was empty of any flower when he offered it to her. Confused, she slipped her fingers against his and let him lead her into the living room and out of the house. The crew was by the fire pit, standing around a box. And when she was close enough, Barret stood aside for her, and she could see inside it. There was a pile of letters nestled in the cardboard container.

Barret set down a giant, blue, plastic water jug and squatted down by the box. His lips formed the words, *Read this one first.* He handed her a letter with Willa's name and return address in the top left corner.

Gen looked around, baffled as she fingered the edge of the white envelope uncertainly. Eden had tears in her eyes, and even Jaxon looked emotional. The others were perfectly quiet, their lips not moving at all. Behind her, Grey wrapped his arms around her chest and kissed her neck as she tore open the top of the envelope.

Inside was a hundred-dollar bill and a letter. Barret snatched the money from her hand and shoved it in the blue jug as Gen read Willa's letter.

Gen, you beautiful, spritely, smexy little earthworm you,

Grey told us what that ass-noggin, Sean, did. I'm glad Vyr ate him. Here is a little money to help for your surgery. I'll send more on the next shipment of worms. I had a bad feeling about that family group, but a good feeling about Grey. Beaston helped.

Love and Wormholes,

Almost Alpha

p.s. sorry I lied about Grey liking olives, blue crayons, juice boxes, and asparagus, but it's a safe bet he likes sixty-nines, long walks in the woods at midnight, tree-sex, green M&Ms, and morning diddles, because he has a penis.

p.p.s You are loved, Gorilla Girl. You always were.

Stunned, Gen sat down by the box. A hundred

dollars for her surgery? That was too much. Barret handed her another envelope. This one was from Bash of the Boarlanders.

The letter was wrapped around three ten dollar bills, and it read, *Sorry about Bangaboarlander. Willa made me do it. She said she would break my leg if I didn't give her the password, and I believe her. She broke Beaston's leg like four times just for fun. Hear good.*

Damon Daye sent her three thousand dollars.

Mom and Dad gave her five hundred.

Torren had pitched in two hundred. His letter just said *You don't suck, Little Monkey.*

Clinton of the Boarlanders gave her sixty-nine dollars, a half-empty pocket shot of whiskey, and a dried dandelion flower.

By the time she opened Beaston and Aviana's letter, she was sobbing, shoulders shaking uncontrollably, because these people truly cared about her being able to hear someday. They cared about her. She sat in the dirt by the fire pit with tears streaming down her face as she read letters from the Ashe Crew, the Breck Crew, the Boarlanders, and Gray Backs. From the Bloodrunners and the

Blackwings.

And when she'd read every letter, and the bottom of the blue jug was covered with the start of her savings for her cochlear implant, Ben stepped forward and rested his hand on the back of her head comfortingly. And then he stuck a wad of cash into the mouth of the jug and made his way toward Jenny and Raif, who waited for him on their porch. Barret shoved a pair of twenties in the jug and gave her head a knuckle sandwich as she laughed emotionally. And one by one, the Red Havoc Crew…her crew…put money in the jug and touched her head. Warmth spread down her body at the affection. Was this strange sensation joy? Was it belonging? She thought so. They weren't well off. The crew struggled with bills and sold moonshine on the side to make ends meet, yet here they were, giving her what they could so she could hear Grey's voice someday.

It meant the whole world.

The family group had taken everything from her, made her feel weak, but Red Havoc had made her strong again.

Grey's contribution took a while. He shoved wad after wad in there, and then signed that it was what he'd made from the bar this week. *All my tips will go to this, Gen. I'm gonna take care of you, and someday, the first words you hear are going to be mine.*

He sat in the dirt and pulled her into his lap. Slowly, she slid her arms around his shoulders and pressed her lips to his. And when she eased back, she mouthed, *What words?*

Piercing blue eyes holding her gaze, he pulled her hand to his chest, right over his pounding heart, and said, "I. Love. You."

With those three all-important words, Gen knew it would happen. She just had this feeling, this gut instinct. Grey wasn't a man who let people down. He was strong, honest, and protected the people he cared about, even when they didn't know it. Her heart swelled with the realization that someday, someway, she was going to hear.

But for now, she was okay with remaining the daughter of silence because Grey loved her—just the way she was.

And the Red Havoc Crew accepted her—just the way she was.

And through Grey's tenderness and patience, she was learning to love herself.

Just the way she was.

RED HAVOC GUARDIAN

Want more of these characters?

Red Havoc Guardian is the fourth book in the Red Havoc Panthers series.

For more of these characters, check out these other books from T. S. Joyce.

Red Havoc Rogue
(Red Havoc Panthers, Book 1)

Red Havoc Rebel
(Red Havoc Panthers, Book 2)

Red Havoc Bad Cat
(Red Havoc Panthers, Book 3)

This is a spinoff series set in the Damon's Mountains universe. Start with Lumberjack Werebear to enjoy the very beginning of this adventure.

About the Author

T.S. Joyce is devoted to bringing hot shifter romances to readers. Hungry alpha males are her calling card, and the wilder the men, the more she'll make them pour their hearts out. She werebear swears there'll be no swooning heroines in her books. It takes tough-as-nails women to handle her shifters.

She lives in a tiny town, outside of a tiny city, and devotes her life to writing big stories. Foodie, wolf whisperer, ninja, thief of tiny bottles of awesome smelling hotel shampoo, nap connoisseur, movie fanatic, and zombie slayer, and most of this bio is true.

Bear Shifters? Check

Smoldering Alpha Hotness? Double Check

Sexy Scenes? Fasten up your girdles, ladies and gents, it's gonna to be a wild ride.

> For more information on T. S. Joyce's work,
> visit her website at
> www.tsjoyce.com